This book is dedicated to Jeremy Corbyn who steadfastly helps the poor, the sick and the homeless.

Preview

After the turmoil created by Victor Salomon on Juniper Island, Piper Lee became involved in searching for three young children who had been missing for two years.

Now in need of some tranquility in her life, she moved to Rainbow Bridge with Calico, Rafi and her best mate Stanley, a golden retriever. They lived in a beach house and had the most wonderful time with new friends and lots and lots of four legged friends.

One day 2Sheds arrived and everything changed. The roller coaster had started all over again.

Chapter 1

If Piper Lee thought of her favourite landscapes in The Earth World, she could find carbon copies of them in the land surrounding Rainbow Bridge.
Saltwater beaches, sweeping hills and dales, untamed woodlands and fresh, sparkling rivers were all in her local vicinity.

The lands around Rainbow Bridge were for the animals and birds that had died on Earth. Nobody or nothing could hurt them here. They were free to live their natural life with no predators of any kind. There was no such thing as eating meat. It was as the old quotation stated,
'The lion shall lie down with the lamb'

For the past year Piper and her little family had been living in the predominantly doggy part of Rainbow Bridge. They lived in a beach house in the dunes. They were there to befriend and enjoy the company of these faithful companions.

There were sleeping shelters for dogs who hung out together. There were individual shelters for dogs who preferred to sleep alone. Every eventuality was catered for.

Piper, Rafi and Calico made sure there was plenty of dog food and plenty of fresh water for them all. Stanley loved the company of the other dogs and could be seen playing ball games with them.

Some of the dogs had a handprint on their right shoulder. This meant that they had a human soulmate who would one day cross the Rainbow Bridge to find them. The reunited friends would then set off for The Lysie Fields and live the life of their choice.

Some Lysie Landers who had never shared their life with a dog in The Earth World and some dogs that never had a human could also get together in Rainbow Bridge.

Other humans who had chosen to live here had beach houses near Piper and they often shared barbecues together in the evenings. They would light a fire on the beach and enjoy each other's company, eat bean burgers, drink beer and sing songs. And the dogs came too.

Chapter 2

One morning, Piper was sweeping the floor of the beach hut when she heard a crashing noise outside. Rafi and Calico had taken the breakfast dishes to the outdoor sink to wash and Piper presumed they had dropped them.

She was correct but when she looked out of the kitchen window she didn't expect to see a man lying on the ground and Stanley sitting on top of him, Calico bumping up and down on the poor man's feet and Rafi performing some sort of tribal dance around him. Even Patch, the miniature donkey was lying across his face.

Piper ran outside and immediately picked up the little donkey, "Bloody hell, what's going on", she exclaimed apologetically.

"I am so sorry. I don't know why they are doing this."

And then she did know!

As she lifted Patrick up, she saw 2Sheds' handsome face underneath. He looked flabbergasted. She picked off Calico who then joined Rafi's dance and called Stanley off. He happily did as he was asked, wagging his tail as he went to join the nitwits.

Piper grabbed 2Sheds's hands as he struggled to stand up. When he was on his feet, she threw her arms around him and kissed him on the lips.

"I didn't think you would be so pleased to see me," he gasped trying to regain some breath in his lungs.

"But it's been so long," Piper squealed with delight.

By now Patch had worked his way through the young man's legs and was awaiting some attention. Both of were still dancing and chanting,

"We want 2Sheds."

Eventually normal life was resumed and Piper remembered that a lady was crossing the bridge at noon to meet up with her dogs.

"Do you fancy coming to the bridge with us?" asked Piper eagerly.

"We have some dogs waiting to meet their human companion."

"Can it wait a while?" quibbled 2Sheds vaguely.

"Of course it can't," laughed Piper.

"Guys, I need Poppy, Sky and Phoebe," Rafi and Calico ran off to the beach calling their names.

Piper took 2Sheds' hand and led him around the beach hut to where a khaki coloured jeep with large windows and a pop up roof was parked.

"Jump in," and Stanley made sure that he was in the middle of the front seat.

" Why does my dog love you so much? He still has your old blue converse boot." said Piper.

"Because we're mates, aren't we Stan?" and 2Sheds climbed in and sat beside the golden retriever.

By now the guys were back with three standard apricot poodles who eagerly jumped in the back of the jeep. They definitely knew what was going on. Calico and Rafi lifted Patch into the back and Piper fastened them in.

She jumped in the front, looked across at 2Sheds and said, "I think you had better use the seat belt."
He did not have time to reply before the jeep stuttered, juddered and jerked away. Calico was laughing and shouted out,
"She always does that. She's not very good at driving."

Their journey took them along wide open spaces until they came to a vast meadow with a river running through it and the Rainbow Bridge stood steadfast and rock solid over the river.

The bridge was naturally rainbow shaped and rainbow coloured. The stones it was built from were tinged with the appropriate colours and sparkled in the sunshine. It was not gaudy or flashy but like an old weathered friend who's mission in life was to bring loved ones together.

Piper stopped the jeep with a judder and a jerk and jumped out while everyone else was making sure their stomachs were still in the right place.

The poodles ran off to the bridge and waited on full alert for signs of their human coming over the bridge. They didn't have to wait long before she was with them. The lady, now in her prime, was ecstatic to be with her girls again.

With a wave of her hand to Piper, she called her dogs and they all walked back across the bridge into their forever lives.

"Ready to go back?" asked Piper.

"First one back to the jeep does the driving", shouted 2Sheds as he started to run.

"Bloody cheek," laughed Piper as she chased after him.

Chapter 3

The afternoon was spent looking after all the dogs and of course, the nitwits made sure that 2Sheds did his share of the work. He tried to tell Piper that he needed time to talk to her,

"Don't worry we can chat tonight," she said. She was preoccupied looking after two little boys who had passed over that afternoon. One was a corgi called Candy and the other was a spaniel cross called Jedi. They were so happy to be fit and healthy again.

"Come on guys, let's go exploring and Piper and Stanley set off over the grasslands with the two dogs racing ahead. "We're staying with 2Sheds," shouted Rafi. "Cool, remember to look after Patch," shouted Piper, as she disappeared from view.

"Can we join the football match on the beach?" asked Calico.

"Sounds good to me but I do need to speak to Piper when she gets back."

The nitwits took little notice and ran off over the sand dunes, whooping and hollering as they went.

When 2Sheds caught up with them, they were with a group of children and adults who were kicking a ball around on the damp sand.

"This is our friend. He is called Eric but we call him 2Sheds." said Calico loudly.

2Sheds smiled and said hi to them.

"You're on our team." added Rafi.

"We're the ones with t-shirts on."

As he spoke four more adults arrived carrying portable goals. Knowing what was going to happen next, Patch took himself back to the sand dunes and curled up to have a snooze.

The game had a referee with a whistle, red and yellow cards and oranges for half time.

2Sheds enjoyed the game and fitted in easily with the comradery of his peers. The youngsters were good fun too. By the time the game finished, Piper and Stan were back.

"Where are your new friends?" asked 2Sheds.

"They stopped off at one of the shelters for some refreshments and probably will get some sleep," she answered. You okay?"

"Yes but I guess I'm ready for a shower?" Piper looked over at her friends,

"We're going back to the beach house. Are you eating out later?"

"Yeah about five." a bronzed guy with sun bleached hair replied.

"See you then" said Piper as they walked away.

"Don't forget Patch," someone shouted.

Chapter 4

By the time everyone showered and sorted themselves out, it was almost five and they all returned to the part of the beach where they usually met up. Here, tree trunks had been hollowed out to form seating with blankets and cushions added for comfort. A fire pit was another feature as was the barbecue.

There were about twenty five people and about forty five dogs. Most of the humans were Lysie Landers apart from Piper and 2Sheds, who were mere mortals. Some were preparing food, others were still kicking a ball around and some were sitting around having a drink and chatting amongst themselves. 2Sheds joined the latter group and joined in with their conversations.

"Piper has told us a lot about you and your rescue work. It is very admirable." said one of the girls.

"It's all down to John Bartlebee and Abednego really. I'm just part of the team." answered 2Sheds.

"How did you all get together? she asked.

"Long story, but when John Bartlebee died, he was furious about the cruelty in The Earth World. He could not let it go and so he decided to do something about it. He heard about a shipbuilder who had built a copy of The Titanic with fellow Lysie Landers.

Once built, they wanted to use the ship for the pursuit of education. They fitted a massive library and equipped the ship throughout like a massive learning centre for all ages.

Lysie Landers who had missed out on a thorough and meaningful education flocked to the ship. Sleeping accomodation was provided and students travelled many worlds as they improved their own knowledge and understanding.

    Eventually John devised ways of rescuing young people from The Earth World. Then if they were willing, he would ask them to return and rescue their fellow humans from poverty and cruelty.

    Lots of other facilities also became available. One of these was The Lysie Fields Registry of births and deaths. The staff would frequently pass on information if children were going to
die because of human cruelty.

    That's how John Bartlebee knew that I had been abandoned as a newborn baby on a beach in France. He set up a rescue operation and I was brought back to Abednego and given a second chance at life."

    2Sheds looked up. He did not know that his story had attracted more listeners. He felt embarrassed.

"They tease me about you and call you Han Solo but now they know what a great job you do." chipped in Piper.
"Not a Skywalker, I'm gutted." grinned 2Sheds. "Don't worry that's all for tonight."

The food was cooked and the beer was flowing so everyone had their fill of the provisions. There were even carrots for Patch.

After the food there was music. Some folk played guitars while others sang. There was dancing and terrible karaoke singing. Piper and 2Sheds laughed, danced together and even jived to Elvis the Pelvis.

They left while they were still able to safely carry the sleeping nitwits back to the beach house and Piper and her family all crashed on her king size bed.

2Sheds found a room with a bed. He pulled off his clothes and disappeared under the duvet until he was woken some hours later by Piper.
"Are you awake Sheds?" she whispered.

"No," he answered bluntly.
"Can you do me a favour?" she continued.
"In the morning," and he nuzzled into the duvet.
"I want to have sex with you now,"
"WHAT!!," he queried, as he raised himself up on one elbow.
"I want to lose my virginity and I can't think of anyone better to lose it with. Move over."
Without further ado, Piper whipped off her t-shirt and clambered into his bed. She cuddled into him.
"I'm not sure I can do this to order," he said.
"Well let's start with kissing and see what happens."
They started kissing until Piper broke away, "Almost forgot." She put her hand over the side of the bed and picked up a towel and pushed it under her bottom.
"Just in case," she added.

"I'm not going to be able to do this in a minute. I'm not a machine."

The deed was done and lasted about twenty minutes. "Not my most sensual encounter. Can I go back to sleep now." "Thanks Shedsie, now I can start my life of debauchery."

Piper slipped out of bed with the towel and he could hear the shower working several minutes later. He smiled and went back to sleep.

He woke up several hours later with the word debauchery foremost in his mind. She must have been joking, he thought as he lay there.

After a while he got up for a pee and noticed Piper asleep on the settee. The rest of the family must still be in her bed, he thought. He went over to the settee and picked her sleepy body up in his arms and carried her back to his bed.

"Now let's do this properly,"
he whispered into her ear.

Chapter 5

The next morning at breakfast Calico said, "Are you two married now?"

"What do you mean?" asked Piper, dreading what she was going to say.

"You slept in bed with 2Sheds. That's what married people do."

"That's because her bed was full of wriggly little bodies," answered 2Sheds, giving Piper a knowing look.

"Anyway I need to talk to Piper for five minutes," he added. "Can you make yourselves busy?"

"Cool," said Rafi, and they went outside before Piper gave them a job to do.

Piper wondered what he was going to say, especially after the perfect ending to their adventures in bed.

He looked ill at ease. I hope he didn't forget to tell me he's married, she thought.

"I've been meaning to tell you something since I arrived here but somehow have never had the chance."

"What is it?" she asked, feeling worried.

"A few days ago, one of the messenger angels came to Abednego and invited John to go with him to a meeting in Heaven."

"What? How do we know he will come back ? Sheds, you should have told me."

"But you were so pleased to see me. I didn't want to spoil the moment."

"Well you have now," She stood up and walked to the window. She watched the nitwits building a camp out of wooden boxes.

"What is the meeting about?" she asked, her face tense with worry.

"I don't know but John was reassured that nothing drastic was going to happen. He will be gone for about a month." 2Sheds got up and walked over to her and rested his hands on her shoulders.

"One month! That's a long bloody meeting." She immediately stopped. Perhaps she shouldn't swear when it came to meetings with messenger angels.

"There's something else," 2Sheds said gingerly.

Piper shrugged off his hands and returned to her chair at the table.

"You had better tell me everything because I'm fearing the worst."

He sat down beside her. "Before the angel arrived, John was planning to take a group of us on a trip to an ancient palace. It's a newly excavated site on Greysands."

"So?" said Piper petulantly.

"Well he still wants us to go and he will meet us there when he comes back."

"If he comes back," she retorted.

"I understand why you're being difficult and I've apologised. When I've told you the significance of this palace, you can decide whether you want to come with us or not."

2Sheds sat back in his chair. He wasn't going to sidestep the issue now.
"What makes this ancient palace of interest to you, are the links between it and life before the destruction of the place we now call Greysands. It should also help us learn about Gogo's ancestors.

Chapter 6

It was while looking through The Lysie Fields Registry that John Bartlebee realised he had fathered a baby in The Earth World. He was shocked to the core that he had been so reckless. The baby was the result of a one night stand when he was a young man travelling through Manchester.

The baby was Piper Lee and he followed her life from afar. There were many things that worried him about her circumstances but nothing that he could do to help her. That is until the night her step father fractured her skull by pushing her down a flight of concrete steps.

Under John's direction, 2Sheds rescued her and she came to live on Abednego. She met up with her grandad, Jack Lee and her beloved golden retriever, Stanley. She was happy for the first time in a long time and even helped 2Sheds with the rescue operations.

Everything was fine until the day she and Stanley were kidnapped by a strange man called Tanic Clay and flown off to the most wretched and desolate land imaginable. This was Greysands.

Everything from the sky above to the land below was covered with fine grey particles with no sign of anyone ever living there.

Piper and Stanley were taken to the only house that could be seen for hundreds of miles. Here she met Amalie and Gogo and they eventually became good friends. Amalie was the lady of the house and Gogo was her dowdy but talented carer.

Piper stayed there for six months before she escaped with her quickly growing family. They arrived back on Abednego with Gogo, a very ill Amalie, a small baby reared by cats, a donkey foal that needed bottle feeding and two cats.

Right from the beginning, Piper knew Gogo was special. She had the most amazing skills and could do anything she put her mind to. She thought nothing of building a working car from a few scrapped vehicles. She was artistic and could sing like an angel.

On Abednego, after a shower and new clothes, Gogo was transformed into a beautiful young woman with golden dreadlocks that fell to her waist.
One day while out walking with Piper, she disappeared through the membrane that

divided The Lysie Fields from Heaven and Piper never saw her again.

Since that time, archaeologists from The Lysie Fields had started excavating a variety of sites on Greysands and were putting together a prehistory of fascinating facts. Large communities had lived there until a colossal environmental disaster had destroyed everything under a mountain of grey sand.

Chapter 7

Piper went quiet on 2Sheds and was mulling over what he had said when Rafi and Calico came running in for refreshments.
"2Sheds wants to know if you want to go on an adventure holiday?" asked Piper, passing the response to the proposal over to the nitwits.
"Yes please," said Calico. "Can we all go?
"Will there be a fun fair?" asked Rafi.

"Not exactly but lots of fun things to do." reassured 2Sheds popping four year old Calico on his knee.

"We've been invited to stay in a palace in a place called Greysands,"

"Not Greysands," said Calico. "We had to escape from there once before."

"I know you think of Greysands as a boring, colourless place where there were no flowers and trees," he soldiered on.

"Piper grew flowers and vegetables?" butted in Calico proudly.

"That's right. She scraped away the grey sand-like stuff and found seeds, bulbs and soil," explained 2Sheds patiently.

"Why do you say 'sand-like?" asked Piper, with no petulance in her voice now.

"Because it has been analysed to contain much more than tiny granules of rock and minerals. A whole civilization seems to have disintegrated into tiny crumbs."

"I don't understand," said Rafi,

"So let's get to the exciting bits," said 2Sheds, not wanting to lose his audience. "We have been invited to stay at a newly excavated palace carved out of pink sandstone. It was built by a friendly and artistic race of people who cared for each other and cared for their environment.
"Does a king and queen live there?" asked Calico, now cuddled into 2Sheds' chest.
"Nobody lives there now and that is why John has arranged for us to stay while the work outside the palace is still going on.
"The fun things for nitwits are warm water springs with fountains and whirlpools. There is an art room where you can paint and make models. And there is a stone staircase with two slides on either side.
"Are you interested now," chipped in Piper. "Yeah,yeah, yeah. What else?"
"There are no bedrooms because there is an open flat roof on the top of the palace where there are tents for you to sleep in

and all the cooking is done around the campfire.

"Can we go now?" asked Rafi.

"Go now?" echoed Calico.

Piper stood up, "First you two need to make sure that every broken cup and dish is picked up from yesterday. We cannot leave a mess for someone else to clear up."
The children jumped to attention but Piper had not finished.

"Then you each need to pack a bag with five pairs of pants, t-shirts, shorts and socks. You will also need two jumpers, one coat and one pair of trainers."

They were gone before she had finished speaking. She turned towards 2Sheds,"Who else will be there?"
"John invited Joram and Maya, Obadiah and Ivy and Marigold said she would like to come,"
" Cool and when are we going,"
" Because I delayed telling you, the others have already gone." admitted 2Sheds. "A

light aircraft is available to fly us from here. I just have to message Abednego and arrange a time."

Unfortunately 2Sheds had reminded her that he had caused this delay in information. She was going to take a pop at him but on second thoughts had decided not to.

"I need to take one of the dogs to Rainbow Bridge soon and then I will have to ask one of the gang to take over for me." she said.

"Do you think that will be a problem?" he asked, glad that they were back on good terms.

"I don't think so because there are always extra people here. It's the perfect place to live. Anyway I'd better go. Guys, can you fetch Bruno for me?"

She went outside with Stan and saw that the nitwits had done a good job of clearing the debris. As she reached the jeep, dear sweet Bruno was bursting with anticipation and joy. Stanley jumped up into the back of the jeep with him, their tails making perfect windscreen wipers.

"Don't forget to pack Stanley's converse boot?" she said as she shuddered and juddered the jeep down the track.

Chapter 8

The light aircraft that took off that evening with Piper and her family was a first time experience for all of them except 2Sheds who had used them during his many rescue missions. Everything went smoothly and they all enjoyed a good night's sleep.

They arrived the next morning on the newly constructed runway outside the designated project area. The archaeologists had not been sure how many dwellings they would find but it was now obvious from first sight that many caves had been scooped out of the lower part of the mountain range.

This was a land of varying landforms including deep canyons and tall waterfalls with pink sandstone structures such as the palace in which they were going to stay. Tracks had been created by the wind and rain carving through them for thousands of years.

The group followed the track that had been created by continual use towards a wide roadway at the base of the mountain range. Everything here was a yellow and orange combination. The sand contained grains of quartz which according to the archeologists was coated with an iron ore which provided it with an orange colour in places.

They had not walked far when they saw two carriages pulled by donkeys coming towards them. As they came closer, Joram could be seen driving one and his younger sister Maya driving the other.

Piper had met Joram when she was working with John to rehome a large group of refugees on Juniper Island. They were all youngsters and Joram's friend, Victor Saloman, had been the original leader of the group.

It turned out that Victor had a vicious nature and had caused no end of trouble for Piper who was the project leader. Eventually Victor was expelled from the island and Piper resigned from her post after questioning her own behaviour in a critical incident.

Joram had supported her throughout the troubled times and there had been a wonderful moment for everyone when the young man had been reunited with his parents and younger sister.

Before travelling to Greysands, the siblings had been in the Earth World where they had been helping Albertina

Westaways adapt her large home in North Devon to a working community for homeless people.

Albertina had been the lady who had looked after the three missing children and saved them from being split up. Without her, the older boys would have been put into care and the younger two probably adopted. The children were now living with their auntie in Australia.

The donkey led carriages stopped beside the group and the brother and sister jumped out to welcome their friends.

Not only did the humans embrace but Patch was so pleased to meet his own kind again that he rubbed his body against them in friendship. Luckily these donkeys seemed pleased to meet him too.

Piper, Rafi and Stanley travelled with Maya and 2Sheds and Calico went with Joram. Patch trotted along with his new mates.

It felt like they were riding through a maze of blank streets made of stone walls until they came out onto a large sandy courtyard in front of a massive pink palace carved into the side of a mountain.
The donkeys pulled up outside.
"You didn't say it was a pink palace" said Rafi, staring at the wondrous building before his eyes.
"That's the colour of the stone," replied Maya. "You can see the same colour running through the rock on this mountain but it seems more concentrated here." She jumped down and held onto the donkey's reins.
    When they were all reunited on the ground, 2Sheds came and put his arm around Piper's shoulders.
"Are you impressed?" he said. "It's incredible that prehistoric people could achieve such perfection."
Piper looked genuinely impressed.

"Joram says the mountains are peppered with dwellings and passages. There are also man-made waterways built for the convenience of the inhabitants," continued 2Sheds.

Once the group had sorted out their luggage, Joram spoke to them, "If it's okay, I will give you a brief tour before we stop for dinner at the top."

"Good idea," said Piper and she turned to the nitwits. "Guys, that means, we won't be going in the bathing pools or painting any pictures until we've had a look around and sorted out our bags."

"Oh no, looking around sounds boring" moaned Calico. "I want to play."

"That's okay," replied Piper. "Let's just do the boring bit quickly."

The friends walked up the stone steps and through the giant doorway that had no door. The daylight poured through onto a spectacular stone staircase that had been carved into the mountain. It led up to a first floor that stretched around half of the inner bedrock. The rest had been chipped away to create a large empty space.

The atmosphere was warm and wet and this was due to the geothermal water baths that sloped off from the base of the stairs and led far back into the depths of the mountain. Lights were lit at strategic points and some were fixed under the water to create a very calm and magical atmosphere. There were even fans on the walls to give a gentle breeze.

Calico and Rafi already had their hands in the water and were trying to catch bubbles from the jets.
"This is so cool," said Rafi.
"It gets even better because there are whirlpools as well." chipped in Maya.

The group followed the flowing curves of the water spa until they could see daylight and saw that there was an outside area, where air seats were positioned in the bubbling water.

"This is a good place to relax in the evenings." said Joram. "Or just float down the lazy river."

"I can't wait to get in," sighed Piper.
"And me." agreed Rafi.
"Let's quickly finish the tour, say hi to the others and leave you to soak in the spa for the rest of the day," said Joram who realised the children were getting restless.

They walked past the entrance to the outside spa and returned on the other side. As they climbed the stone staircase, Calico pointed out the two polished slides on either side and Piper was relieved to see that they had safety.

The upper level was divided into three main areas. The area on the left was the painter's studio. The area on the right was for the sculptors. In the middle was a vast community room which opened onto an open air living space.

As soon as Calico looked inside, she could see Marigold sitting cross legged at a low table preparing food. The young girl jumped up immediately to see her friends. The others followed.

Marigold was one of the first people that Piper had met when she arrived on Abednego. She was the one that first showed her around the ship and to Piper's surprise turned out to be the same girl who entered The Lysie Fields with John Bartlebee.

When Piper returned from captivity in Greysands, it was Marigold that helped her look after Calico and Patch. That was four years ago and they had remained close ever since. Marigold was now fifteen years old and blossoming into a beautiful teenager.

It turned out that she was preparing pizzas for lunch. The nitwits put their favourite toppings on the two she was working on as the young girl took another two pizzas out of a sturdy brick oven positioned against the stone wall.

"I hope you're hungry because I've made plenty," said Marigold. "Help yourself. The table is laid."

A long wooden table with chairs around it stood at the far end of the roof which had a view of the landscape at the side of the palace. There was no view at the back, just a continuation of the mountain rising into the sky and out of sight. It looked impossible to climb.

Marigold put the last two pizzas in the oven, while everyone took their place at the table.

"Sorry we're late," said a voice from the doorway. It was Obadiah holding a carved wooden box. Ivy was following close behind.

"Obie, Obie Obie !" shouted Calico as she bounced up and down on her chair. Obie put the box down and walked around the table giving everyone a hug or a high five. Ivy gave everyone a wave as she found a seat.

"What have you got there?" asked 2Sheds.

"Don't really know because I can't open it? But I have a funny feeling that it's something that the archaeologists missed." The carvings were patterns of various shapes with possibly initials in the center.

Obadiah quickly put his newly found treasure under his seat as a new face came through the glass doors.

"Sorry to butt in," said the man.

"Not at all," replied Joram standing up.

"Guys, this is Frank Bennet. He's the main man on the dig and will keep us updated on what is being discovered."

Joram turned to Frank, " You are welcome to join us. As you can see we have plenty of food."

"Don't mind if I do," said Frank, beaming at Marigold who had brought in the last two pizzas.

A lot of cutting, slicing and scooping then took place as everyone passed around dishes and plates and everyone started to munch through pizzas with coleslaw, pizzas with salad, pizzas with chips or pizza with a bit of everything.

"Are you Piper?" asked Frank as he sat down in the empty seat beside her.

"Yes I am and it's good to meet you Frank," smiled Piper. "Your job must be very interesting."

"Well it's because of you that I'm here. If you hadn't scraped back the grey particles and discovered the dormant seeds in the soil, none of this might have happened for a long time. Greysands was always a no go area."

2Sheds who was sitting opposite raised his eyes in a 'here we go' gesture. He could see that these two were going to get on famously. They even looked suited. Frank had longish hair and a beard. He dressed scruffy and had that hippy look about him. 2Sheds wasn't going to get a word in edgeways.

When they eventually did stop talking, Piper helped Calico pour herself a drink.

Frank turned towards Joram, "I came to let you know that we had another sighting of our little friend with the dreads last night."

"Where was he?" asked Joram.

"Milly caught a glimpse of him around our food tent but when she got there, he was gone."

"Hang on," chipped in Piper. "Will our children be safe to wander around?

I thought the site was deserted."

"We're not absolutely sure there is somebody. Some of our group have thought they have seen a young lad but nothing for sure. John was going to tell you." continued Frank.

"That's my fault," said 2Sheds. "I forgot to tell you."

It was Piper's turn to raise her eyes in exasperation .

"Guess you're on the first security detail Sheds," she said pointedly. How old is this phantom boy supposed to be?"

"Possibly about nine years old. We're really not sure." replied Frank. "I hope this hasn't worried you Piper. Hopefully we can sort it out very soon."

He stood up. "I had better be on my way. Thanks for the delicious food Marigold."

"Yes those pizzas are the best ever," added 2Sheds, putting another slice onto his plate.

"You are my number one chef !"

Piper was surprised to see Marigold blush and look away to regain her composure. She was equally surprised to see Maya miming a kiss with full pouty lips at Marigold. Did they have a crush on 2Sheds?

When Frank was gone, Piper asked about the sleeping arrangements.

"It's been difficult to make a decision because we only have two tents." said Ivy, sensing Piper's change of mood.

"They look lovely," added Piper, trying to sound more upbeat and cheery.

"It's a bit boring but we thought of one tent for the girls and the other for the boys. Do you think that will be ok?" said Obie as he lifted the wooden box back onto the table.

"That's fine" smiled Piper as she saw 2Sheds looking not quite so fine anymore. I bet he was thinking of a different set up, she thought.

"Right I'm off to see if I can unlock this box," said Obie. "I would love to find out about the people who created this amazing place."

"Can we go in the whirlpool now?" asked Rafi.

"Well I'd better sort out our bedding first," said Piper.

2Sheds stood up. "Do you trust me to take them?" he said, half expecting her to say no. But she didn't.

"They'll need to take their swimming gear out of their backpacks."
Suddenly the nitwits were gone.
Somethings Piper didn't have to say twice!
And Patch had gone with them.
2Sheds gave Piper a peck on the cheek.

Chapter 9

The two bell shaped tents were candy striped with an entrance formed by an A frame and guy robes for stability. Coloured bunting decorated the front.

The tents had been placed at either end of the rooftop. Piper thought this was to make sure that the people in one tent did not disturb the other tent and vica versa.

She went into the candy striped tent and saw that it contained the girl's luggage. The setting was bohemian with a scattering of rag rugs, indian drapes and embroidered cushions.

Five sleeping bags with pillows and an extra blanket lay from the central pole to the outside. It looked like a clock with multiple hands. Piper chose the place by the entrance and made room for Calico beside her. When the others came back, she would ask them to move around a little bit more to make room for Stanley and Patch.

After dropping their backpacks, she dropped Rafi's in the boys' tent. She did not choose a sleeping bag for him in case he wanted to sleep in her tent.

Before going in search of the nitwits, Piper wanted to have a look in the two studios. She and Stan went into the sculpting studio first. There were stone statues of a fine looking man and woman who looked regal and clearly outshone their peers.

There were busts of them too. On closer inspection, Piper could see damage to the genetic dreadlocks and wondered if the crowns had been removed with a chisel. There were also realistic wood carvings of animals such as dogs, foxes, cows and sheep. Piper wondered how old the artwork was. She must remember to ask Frank.

In the middle of the floor, there were a few ongoing projects and Piper wondered who had started them. Were they ancient or modern?

Next she and Stan walked across to the painting studio. As she walked through the arched doorway, Piper stopped in bewilderment. Her breath seemed to have left her body. The stone walls were adorned with sensational works of art, all seemingly as rich in colour as the day they were painted. There were oil paintings, water-colours, pastels and charcoal drawings. The walls were covered in them with very few spaces.

Piper noticed a large painting had been removed and in the space where it had hung, was a tunnel dug into the stone.

She peered inside to see a space full of paintings packed closely together.

The one thing that totally overwhelmed her was that many of the paintings depicted the land full of domestic animals and rich vegetation. There were fields and trees and meadows full of unusual flowers. The courtyard outside was a garden growing large vegetables, fruits and flowers.

"What a difference Piper, I share your amazement." She turned to see Obadiah sitting at a table by a window. Ivy was beside him trying to open the lock of the wooden box with what looked like a kirby grip.

"Is this what this place used to look like?" asked Piper nervously. She was afraid it was all a big hoax.

"It certainly seems to be the case," replied Obie. "When you think of what you found under the grey particles and subsequently grew into healthy plants, it suggests that some catastrophe of epic proportions happened to the whole of Greysands."

There was a click and Obie stopped talking and looked over to Ivy, who was smiling triumphantly.

"Done it?" he asked hopefully.

"Always trust a kirby grip to pick a lock." she laughed.

She slid the box over to Obie and moved in closer to have a look at what was inside. Piper did the same.

Obadiah slowly lifted the lid and the most amazing fragrance filled the air.
It was musty but sweet. The box was lined with deep green felt and at the top was a layer of delicate purple and yellow pressed flowers.

Very carefully, Obie lifted the delicate flowers out of the box and laid them on the table. They looked like primroses but were bigger and were definitely the source of the musky sweet perfume.

He then carefully slid his hand down the sides of the box and took out several books. They looked yellowed by age and the top one was decorated with the purple flowers on the cover. The paper was handmade with crinkly edges. The books were held together with a red satin ribbon.

Obadiah carefully lifted the books out of the box and undid the ribbon. He opened random pages of the top book and there was writing with some illustrations. It looked like Latin which made sense as it was known to have originated in 700 BC and influenced many other languages.

"This reminds me of the work of a young person," said Piper, straightening up.

"You may be right," said Ivy. "I think Obie will have a laborious job translating them. Perhaps it would be easier for Frank's team," she said, already knowing what Obadiah would say next.

"Just give me a day or two and we might find some interesting new facts about our holiday home,"
said Obie, not realising he was being teased.
Ivy and Piper gave each other a knowing look. This was what Obie did best.
"Well good luck guys. Stanley and I are off to the hot springs. While Piper was changing into her bathing costume, Stanley enjoyed sinking into the vibrant water and swimming off to find 2Sheds and the nitwits.

When Piper found them, they were sitting on air cushions at an even distance from each other. They were throwing a tennis ball to each other but if they dropped it, the penalty was to eject the air cushion and try to hang on while it rose to the surface.
They were hooting with laughter.

Only 2Sheds could invent a game like that, thought Piper as she stayed out of sight to watch them.

She could easily see why Maya and Marigold thought he was a heart-throb. He was handsome with a good body and a gorgeous smile. In fact she had never seen him look as perfect as he did then. Just messing around with her family. Stanley had loved him from the first moment they had met and had always treasured the old blue converse boot he had nicked in the early days.

Piper thought of Ty Clay, the man she had grown to love despite their early history. She had enjoyed every day she had spent with him on Juniper Island and never wanted to be separated from him. Unfortunately a summons from a higher order had suddenly taken him away from her and he was now sailing the farthest oceans of this world searching out the waifs and strays and offering them comfort and support. She would never see him again in her lifetime.

Once spotted by the troops, Piper was thrust into the game which had degenerated into mayhem.

Two competitors now had to hit the button at the count of three and strive to stay on the cushion the longest before toppling over.

When it was Piper against 2Sheds, the pair came to the top at the same time and spontaneously grabbed each other.

They kissed on the lips in the joy of the moment. When Piper looked up, she saw Marigold and Maya walking past with mouths agog at the site before them!

Chapter 10

The next morning Piper found herself back in the hot springs with Calico. Everyone else had chosen other activities but the little girl was keen to play in the warm water in the outside area. For some unknown reason, she had slept fretfully in the tent and Piper thought she would go along with what she wanted to do. It might ease any anxieties she was having.

Stanley had gone exploring with 2Sheds, Joram and Rafi. He would enjoy that. Patch had been dropped off at the donkey paddock where he mooched around with his mates. Unlike the incident at Juniper Island, all these guys were friendly and there seemed little danger of him getting bitten again.

While Calico was outside playing with her toy animals, Piper sat by the doorway on an air cushion. She had a large cold drink and was listening to a history podcast about life before Christ. She had been blown away by her visit to the art studios and the discovery of the books in the carved box.

After a while she became aware of two people sitting around the corner from her. She turned down the volume on her headphones and could hear Maya and Marigold having a good old tete a tete with plenty of giggling involved.

Piper was intrigued and moved a bit closer.

"I wanted to come on this trip to see more of him. See him when he's relaxing," said Maya.

"Do you mean more of his body?" said Marigold and they both dissolved into giggles.

Surely they don't mean 2Sheds, thought Piper. He is far too old for them.

"I love him," cooed Maya.

"So do I," sighed Marigold.

Bloody hell this has got to stop, thought Piper but realised there was nothing she could do. They were just growing up and had a crush on 2Sheds.

Piper could now hear Calico talking animatedly to someone so she slid back to the entrance and called out.

"Who are you talking to?"

"My new friend," answered Calico.

"What's his name?" asked Piper affectionately. Her last imaginary friend had been Puff the Magic Dragon and it had been hard work finding enough room for him to sleep in her bed.

"Maximus Mudpuddle." she shouted back. Piper took a drink and then realised what her daughter had said. The drink shot back out again, as it dawned on her what that name meant.

Maximus was a Latin name!

Taking out her muted earphones, Piper went outside to see Calico sitting by herself with her toy animals in a wooden boat.

"Has Maximus gone?"

"Yes, he was shy of you." answered Calico.

"Did he give you the boat?" Piper asked.

"No but he said I could use it. I have to leave it here for him to pick up later."

"That was kind of him. Shall we go now? I want to show you the paintings in the art studio."

"Okay, I'll leave my animals here for Maximus."

Calico placed the boat on the stone ledge and started to swim back to the changing rooms. Once dressed, Calico raced up to the art room,
"Wow, Wow, Wow," she exclaimed as she spun around looking at the large paintings. "Do you think Maximus painted one of them?"
"Who did you say?" said a voice behind them.

They turned around to see Obadiah still sitting at the table with his laptop and the pile of journals.

"Calico, will you tell Obie about your new friend?"

"Can I do a painting first?" asked the little girl.

Piper steered her towards the table.
"You tell Obie and I'll find a canvas and some paints.

When Piper came back to the table, she found Obie fascinated with the never ending details rattling out of such a small child. As soon as she made room for Calico on the table, she stopped talking and started painting.

"What do you make of that?" asked Piper. "She has either met a time traveller or an ancestor of the original founders of The Gratitude Settlement" answered Obadiah in such an unequivocal way, she felt shivers down her spine.
"What do you mean?" she asked warily, unsure of what she was going to be told.
"People often gained a surname from the job they did. The Mudpuddles constructed mud huts, which were often used for animal shelters. Likewise The Burntwoods excelled at making charcoal and so it continued.
" Okay that makes sense but what were you calling this place?" asked Piper.
"The Gratitude Settlement. I saw this name in some of Frank's notes and now I find it in the first journal. The palace is called Gratitude and the people are called

Gracious Angels. Their name laterly changed to Grey Angels as the native community were displaced and presumably split up."

"And Maximus is a grey angel?" asked Piper, wide eyed and incredulous of what she was hearing.

"And Gogo, I suspect. These people were peaceful and thrived on the creative arts. They were naturally very clever and extremely skillful." added Obie.

"Sounds like Gogo to me. She could put her hand to anything and be successful. From keeping house to nursing Amalie to mending cars. She was a true whizz kid," Piper said emotionally. She had enjoyed her time with the young woman who had dusty dreadlocks and drab clothes when she first met her.

"Do you want to see my painting?" asked Calico, holding it up for them to see. And there he was, Maximus Mudpuddle with dreadlocks down to his waist. He only wore trousers but appeared to wear his hair as a jacket.

"That's exactly right, Calico."

Obie turned to Piper, "If you look at the paintings on the wall, you will see that the men plaited together the dreads that meet at the sides of the body. When they were joined under the arms they formed a rough and ready waistcoat."

"I think we have some interesting news to tell the others," smiled Piper.

Chapter 11

A big cast iron cooking pot hung from a tripod over the fire. It was full of a delicious smelling vegetable soup. Marigold and Maya had spent the afternoon preparing it. Joram had also been busy making numerous loaves of bread in the stone ovens.

Everyone congregated at the large dining table and the soup was ladled out.

Calico sat beside Piper with her painting propped against the side of her chair.
The conversation at the table was general and upbeat with someone suggesting a game of football in the outer courtyard later.

When Calico thought the meal was nearly over, she stood up on her chair.
"I have something important to show you all." She beckoned for Piper to pass her the painting.
"Eh- emmm, everybody " This is my new friend. His name is Maximus Mudpuddle. He is very handsome and he is real."
She moved her picture around so that everyone could have a good look at him.
"He is very handsome," beamed Marigold.
"I wish I could meet him, added Maya.
"Would he like a game of footy later on?" laughed 2Sheds good-naturedly.
"I can tell you don't believe me, which is mean of you as I am too old to have make-believe friends. I'm a big girl now."

Obadiah stood up. "Shame on you all because this has really happened."

" She met him this morning in the spa. He lent her his wooden boat to put her toy animals in." chipped in Piper.

"Do you think this is the lad that Frank referred to last night?" asked Joram.

"Yes, he could be or there may be others." Obie sat down and continued. "We have managed to open the wooden box and there is a pile of journals inside. They are written in a language similar to Latin and it will take me a while to try and translate them but it seems that they contain a history of what happened here and possibly the rest of Greysands."

2Sheds got up with his dinner dishes. "Well I'm very sorry Calico that I doubted your story and am wondering if I could be in your team for the football match please."

"Am I choosing a team?" she beamed.

"And me?" asked Rafi.

"Come on then, last one down the slide makes supper!"

"But you always lose," shouted Calico as the two nitwits ran to the top of the slides, sat on the cushions and whizzed down. Smiling to himself, 2Sheds sauntered along behind them.

"It works every time!" he grinned. It will be all set up by the time we get there.

"Anyone want to swap washing up duties?" asked Maya hopefully.

"I'll do a double whammy if you do two of mine?" offered Piper who fancied some time to herself.

The girls willingly agreed and ran off after 2Sheds.

Ivy stood up, "Come on Obadiah Johns, you could do with some exercise." She gave him no option and she bundled him off into the kitchen and down the stairs.

"Looks like it's you and me," said Joram.

" I'll be okay, not so many dishes when it's soup. I also have an ulterior motive. I want a quiet look at the first journal."

Joram smiled and got up from the table. "So fun and games in the spa afterwards could be a good suggestion from your point of view."

"A brilliant idea. Thanks Joe." She hadn't called him that before and was slightly embarrassed. Where did that come from?.

Loading the newly plugged in dishwasher was a doddle. The renovators had done a good job of adding modern equipment to the palace. It certainly made life easier.

Soon Piper was sitting at the table in the art studio. Obadiah had commandeered it for his project and there were files and books piled high.
The space in front of his chair was empty but the carved wooden box lay within arms reach.

Piper put on gloves and carefully opened the box. She was only going to look at the book that Obie had been working on. She put it on the table and sat down. It was obviously a journal that had been very carefully made with neat hand sewn binding to keep all the pages in the right order.

The first page had a pen and ink drawing of the palace. It looked very splendid with lush vegetation all around it. Obadiah had told her that the Gracious Angels had developed a complex irrigation system which piped water to where it was needed and none was wasted.

The illustrator had used pastel crayons to add colour and every page had a protective layer between them.

On other pages, Piper could observe the simple clothes of the people with drawings of their daily life. Everyone had dreadlocks, even the babies!

"You look busy," said a voice from the doorway.

It was Frank. Piper felt caught out.
"Me and Obie found some journals and thought we'd try and translate them."
She thought she sounded like she was still at school.

"Looks like an interesting find. Can I have a look?
"Of course, we thought we would go through them chronologically," she waffled.
"Good idea," he said as he seemed to disappear into the pages of the journal. It was at that moment that Obadiah walked into the room.

"Frank is interested in the work we are doing," said Piper in a way that hopefully suggested there wasn't a problem.
"That's good. The translating is proving a bit tricky," added Obie as he joined them at the table.

Frank looked up, "Where did you find the box?"
"Just under that stone ledge. The space goes back further than you realise.

You haven't seen it then?" asked Obie.
"No, I missed out there but I won't spoil your fun. I'll be back for a daily update though ……..

Frank was stopped mid sentence by Calico and Rafi running in …..

"Patch is missing. He's not with the other donkeys, squealed Calico.

"What shall we do?" cried a worried Rafi.

"Not again. How can one little donkey keep getting into trouble." added Obie.

   Piper stood up and pulled out her phone. "After the incident at Juniper Island, Doc Roger put a tracker on him, so if I turn on the app on my phone, we should see where he is."

   They all waited while the information came onto the screen.

"Bloody hell, I don't understand the diagram or the directions," said Piper.

"Pass it here, I should be able to work it out."

Piper passed over her phone. Immediately Frank could see that Patch was not far away but what puzzled him was that the donkey was in one of the caves.

"I bet he's with Maximus Mudpuddle," said Calico looking relieved.

"What did you say?" asked Frank somewhat abruptly.

"I think Calico met one of the grey angels this morning.

"She most certainly did," said an astonished Frank. "The Mudpuddles were an ancient clan who made mud houses. There were many other clans such as The Redvines who produced wine, The Hammerstones who made tools to name but a few."

"To change the subject," chipped in Piper." I think the doc fitted a miniscule camera into one of Patch's eyebrows.

You should be able to open it on the app.

"Wow, he seems to be sleeping on a dreadlock pillow," laughed Frank as he passed the phone back to Piper to see the image.

"I told you," sang Calico triumphantly. "Maximus will bring him back in the morning."

"Well there you go Frank. I love a happy ending." laughed a relieved Piper.

"And I must go," he said. "I have a meeting with my fellow archaeologists. I hope you don't mind me telling them about the journals and Calico's meeting with our very own gracious angel.

As Frank left, a concerned 2Sheds arrived looking for Calico and Rafi.

"Well, what happened to Patch? I thought you would have returned to let me know."

"He's in Max's cave and Calico says that he will bring him back in the morning" reported Rafi.

"If not, the tracker is working so we will be able to find him easily enough." added Piper.

"All good news then. You two, off to the baths now. I want a quick word with Piper." With that 2Sheds pulled Piper out onto the roof where they were alone.

"Guess what," he said."

"You're a numpty."

"A numpty that has found us a cosy little love nest," he said enthusiastically.

He looked so happy, it made her feel happy too.

"We'll have to find someone in our tents to keep an eye on the nitwits." she said.

"That won't be a problem, will it?" He was holding her close now.

"I suppose this will mean that we will be seen as an item." she teased.

"Sounds good to me," and he kissed her. Piper was amazed at how good it felt.

Chapter 12

As it started to get dark, everyone gathered around the fire pit.
The nitwits were ready for bed and munching their way through big bowls of cereal. They were making each other laugh with silly jokes which didn't really make sense but they were enjoying it.
"What is a sort of cat called?" asked Calico.
" Piddles" laughed Rafi.
Hoots of uncontrollable laughter.
"What is a sort of pig called?" asked Rafi.
"Pongs " stuttered Calico
Both nitwits dissolved into giggles.
 2Sheds jumped up. "Okay guys, maybe time to do something different. Maybe it's time you learnt to play a video game?"

"Oh please be Mario," cried Rafi.

"Maybe, but first I have a favour to ask. Piper and I would like to shoot off for a couple of hours.

"Ooooooooh!" laughed the nitwits.

"Where are you going?" asked the ever nosey Calico.

Piper did not expect this and wondered what 2Sheds would say.

"I've found a cosy cave where we can share a picnic and a bottle of wine and talk about stuff."

Piper saw Marigold and Myra look at each other horrified. She hoped they wouldn't be too disappointed but there you go. What's a girl to do?.

Ivy was the first to volunteer, "I'll sort out the game and both of them can sleep in the same tent tonight," said Ivy. "I expect Stanley will keep guard."

"Where's the cave?" butted in Calico.

"That's a secret" smiled 2Sheds.

2Sheds went into the kitchen and came back with his backpack and 2 rolls of camping foam.
"Are you ready ?" he said to Piper.
"So we're not getting dressed up?" she replied.
"No, we're okay as we are."
"I'll just say bye to Stan and she looked around for the nitwits but they had already run after Ivy. She told her dog that she wouldn't be long and asked him to look after the nitwits. He dutifully obeyed and went off to find them.
Taking her hand, 2Sheds led Piper down the stone stairs and into the hot springs.
"I'm just going to take a quick shower," he said.
"Me two," agreed Piper.
Within minutes he was finished and hurrying her to come out. "Just wrap the towel around you."

She did as he said and picked up her bundle of clothes. They both walked to the opening where Calico had been playing earlier and went outside. In front of them was a ledge of sandstone protruding over the water below. 2Sheds took Piper's hand and guided her up the incline to the left of the entrance. It was a tricky climb but there were hand holds carved out of the stone on one side.

When they reached access to the ledge, 2Sheds walked ahead of her and seemed to disappear.

When she got closer, she saw an entrance to a cave and bending her head, she went inside. It was the size and shape of a two man tent. 2Sheds was lighting some tea lights in various glass containers. He unrolled the mats and pulled across a curtain that had been rigged up across the entrance.

Piper felt her body throbbing in anticipation of what was to come. She

walked over to the man who was kneeling there, waiting for her. She let the towel slip to the ground and knelt down beside him. They started to kiss and their surroundings very quickly slipped away.
They did not stop to eat their picnic,
They did not drink the wine,
They did not even speak.
They were learning to make beautiful and delicious love to each other and it was all consuming.

Three hours later they woke from sleep and found their bodies interlaced. They still did not speak but just lay there enjoying the harmony of the moment. When they eventually moved, they slipped down to the hot springs and sitting in the water, they shared the wine and found themselves ravenously hungry for the bag of peanuts that 2Sheds found in his bag.

They shared their inner secrets about themselves. Piper said she had been gutted when Gogo innocently told her about the sexual encounter beteen him and herself. She also said that she had travelled to Winchester with the sole purpose of looking for him.

    2Sheds told her that he had not returned to Abednego because he felt guilty of having that one night stand. He also said that he had hastily left Juniper Island after they had found the three missing children because he had seen her with Ty Clay. Little did he know then that Ty had come to say goodbye to Piper.

It was late when the young lovers returned to their sleeping quarters where everything was quiet. Stanley was lying in the entrance to the tent in which the children were sleeping. As soon as he saw them, he came over wagging his tail. He said hello to Piper first but very quickly went over to 2Sheds and gently took his wrist in his mouth and tried to lead him over to the children's tent.

"Sorry Stan, I can't sleep in the girl's tent," said 2Sheds quietly but still the dog persisted and did not let go of him.

Being a nervous nellie, Piper instantly thought something was wrong.

"Okay, you take a peek inside and I'll wait outside incase I'm needed."

Stanley, with his tail wagging, proceeded to take 2Sheds to the entrance. Piper could see that there was a night light glowing inside and with a racing heart beat went inside.

"Well ?" said 2Sheds, two minutes later.

Piper came out, "I think you had better see this for yourself."

Totally confused, he moved the canvas to see inside. There was no way that he would want to be seen as a peeping Tom and was astonished at the scene before him. In their absence, the three girls had moved out. A double mattress had been placed in the tent with Piper's and 2Shed's sleeping bags zipped together and placed on top.

The nitwits were asleep in their sleeping quarters on either side of the double bed. Stanley had a bed at the bottom of the bed and Patch had a bed beside Calico.

"I guess they think we're an item." said 2Sheds, already taking off his outer clothes to get into bed.

"But we told them that we were just going to talk about stuff,"

"I don't think they believed that for one minute," laughed 2Sheds.

"Let's get some sleep, you've worn me out."

Chapter 13

After working his way through the first journal, Obadiah was finding the translating easier as he discovered familiarities and patterns in the texts. The first journal described a prosperous time in Gratitude's history.

The community successfully grew healthy crops. They reared cows and goats for dairy products and sheep for their wool. They produced excellent wine and honey that merchants travelled long distances to purchase. A barter system was introduced and richly coloured material, rice and a multitude of herbs and spices became available to the angels.

All was well in the community with visitors enjoying the hospitality of their guests. They enjoyed the fine quality food and musical entertainment in a richly artistic setting with the hot springs as an added luxury.

The second journal began with Balbina's handwritten report. She had witnessed the good times.

"I woke early this morning to see the dawning of a new day. I dressed quickly and went outside. My father and brother were just finishing milking the cows and I helped lead them back to their field. It was market day and we would soon be taking our produce into Gratitude to sell or exchange with our neighbours. Merchants from out of the area were already camped on the plains. They would have goods to sell and hopefully new dress material to tempt us with.

    This was always a joyous occasion with laughter and good humour. There would be space in front of the palace for singing and dancing and when the stalls were empty, a banquet would be laid out on the open top roof and we would party until we could party no more.

Later in the journal, Cassia sums up the end of the good life.

" We had a good life until the blue veined men arrived and persecuted us.

They killed our leaders and mentors.

They slaughtered our animals and ate them.

They drank our wine to excess and became monsters.

They stole our young people because they were different.

I have to run away."

Chapter 14

Calico woke up to the sound of Patch braying his head off at the bottom of the stone steps. She ran down to get him and escorted him back to their tent and into her bed.

She looked at everyone and said, "I guess we're a family now."

2Sheds opened one eye, "Oh no, I thought I was having a bad dream."

Piper smiled but kept her eyes closed.

Just then they heard Ivy outside the tent, "Don't forget Sheds that you and I are on cooking duty this morning. We have a load of pies to cook."

"Meet you in the kitchen," he replied as he rolled over to hug Piper.

Thirty minutes later, 2Sheds was drinking coffee and weighing out the flour for the first batch of pies and quiches. Forty five minutes later, Piper popped in to say that she was taking the nitwits to find the lake which had formed in a sandstone basin further along the mountain range.

"Apparently it's the size of an adult swimming pool," said Piper.

"Is it safe?" asked 2Sheds.

" I should think so. Joram and Obie are coming with us so we will be well looked after. I will leave Patch with his mates in the courtyard."

"Have fun" added Ivy, as she looked up from grating a large block of cheese. "Remember to text some photos."

"After Piper had gone, 2Sheds stopped weighing out the flour and picked up his cup of coffee. He turned to Ivy, "Whose idea was it to marry us off then?"

"Mine and Obie's. Do you wish we hadn't done it?"

"No, not at all. I love them all dearly. Piper changed on Juniper Island and I feel like

I've lost a part of her. I suppose I'm still unsure of her true feelings for me."

Ivy stopped grating cheese and looked at him, "I think she became her own person on the island. She had a very hard job controlling Victor Saloman. He was out to make life very difficult for her."

"But to attempt to cut his ear off Ivy, that's brutal," cut in 2Sheds, starting to open up on feelings he had kept deep with him.

Realising that, Ivy was careful about what she said next. "I expect you would have acted similarly though."

2Sheds thought for a minute, "Yes I most certainly would but that's different."

"Why?"

"Because she's a girl," said 2Sheds, finally putting his feelings in words. "And then to fall for Tanic Clay of all people. That took the biscuit !"

"They were happy together. I think Ty was having the young life he had never experienced and perhaps Piper was enjoying the dad that she had never had. It definitely wasn't a sexual affair." 2Sheds swigged down the rest of his coffee, "And I messed her about and wasn't there to support her."

Ivy picked up the cheese grater. "The thing to remember is that Piper has become her own woman now and doesn't look to lean on any man."
"And that's my problem Ivy, I want to look after her."

The two friends stopped their conversation and carried on with their pie making. When the first batch was cooked and cooling down on the kitchen table, 2Sheds took the second batch out to the ovens.
When he came back into the kitchen, Ivy wasn't there but he instantly noticed a trail of pastry leading out onto the landing. What was going on ?

He looked across to the table and a large chunk of the homity pie nearest the edge was missing. It had not been sliced off but torn apart roughly and pieces of potato and leek left sticking out.

It must be Maximus, he thought and followed the trail into the pottery studio. The trail ended in front of a small open window. 2Sheds brushed the remaining crumbs off of the ledge. He looked out at a vast open space. The depth of the drop to the ground was huge. Looking to the sides, there were no hand holds. Just a very long way to fall. The distance from the window to the flat top was over ten feet with nowhere to hold on. The boy could not have climbed out of this window and survived.

　　He ran back to the kitchen to find Ivy attempting to rescue the rest of the pie.

"What happened here?"

"I think it must be Calico's new friend. I followed the trail of crumbs to the window in one of the studios but he seems to have disappeared out of the window."

"Ah, that solves a mystery. Come and see this." said an enlightened Ivy.

She went back outside and over to the sturdy new flagpole that the archeologists had erected. Around the base of the pole was a long piece of rope tied with several knots.

"Do you think if I dropped this rope over the edge of the wall, it would reach that window you were telling me about ?"

2Sheds looked over the wall, "And a bit more. It probably reaches the window below it as well."

" I expect there are a few more escape routes dotted around the palace," said Ivy.

Grinning to himself at the escapology methods of the young gracious angel, 2Sheds walked into the kitchen just in time to see Maximus standing on a chair taking his pen knife from the top shelf.

2Sheds had left it out of reach of small hands before he started baking pies.

"Be careful Maximus, the blade is very sharp."

At the sound of a voice, the boy jumped down, accidentally pressing the catch that released the blade.

"Just drop it, Maximus. I don't want you to cut yourself.

The boy took flight with the knife in his hand. He ran to the top of the stone steps and jumped onto the cushion at the top of the slide.

"Oh shit !" cried out 2Sheds, as he gave chase, dreading what might happen. To his horror, the boy surfed down the slide standing up. At the bend he crouched low and jumped off the end, landing in the stone doorway. He was still in one piece and 2Sheds decided not to pursue the chase.

By the time he reached the doorway, the boy was out of sight and the knife had been discarded on the top step. 2Sheds picked it up and checked the blade for blood. It was clean and with a sigh of relief, he closed away the knife and put it away in his pocket.

He heard Ivy calling him so he returned to the kitchen to tell her about his blood curdling experience.

"I expect he will keep his distance for a while," said Ivy. "He will think we will be out to get him now."

2Sheds thought about the incident, "What a shame that we haven't been able to develop a relationship with him. This is so unnecessary."

The rest of the pie making session was uneventful and the two cooks even had time for a soak in the hot springs and a relaxing snooze on the sunbeds.

Peace and quiet was shattered when the nitwits returned and wanted to play Super Mario.

"You've started something now?" quipped Piper as she walked past.

At the communal meal, 2Sheds told everyone about his encounter with Maximus. Calico was disappointed that she might not see him again.
"I was hoping he would be my boyfriend," she said wistfully.

Chapter 15

Maximus was not seen again for a week and when they did see him, it was not in the best circumstances. Everyone was in the palace. Piper and 2Sheds were preparing a roast dinner whilst the others were relaxing on the rooftop.

Piper had suggested inviting Frank to the meal so she, Calico and Stan had popped out to invite him. It was while they were gone that the drama unfolded.

A strange clanking noise could be heard coming up the stone steps. It sounded like a machine that needed oiling. It turned out

to be a small infantry battalion of about twenty soldiers,
all looking worn out with threadbare uniforms. They carried their rifles on their shoulders and were led by a lieutenant colonel who creaked as she walked. Her hair was cut in a grey bob and she had a hooked nose.

    The unusual sight walked straight past 2Sheds in the kitchen and onto the open roof. Joram stood up to intercept them and saw that the soldiers in the middle of the procession were carrying a wooden cage and in the cage sat Maximus Mudpuddle.

    The lieutenant colonel turned to her troops,
"At ease," she announced. The four soldiers who carried the cage on long poles on their shoulders put it down on the ground and the rest of the soldiers lowered their rifles.

Joram faced the woman, "Why is the boy in a cage?" he asked fiercely. The soldiers immediately raised their rifles to a shooting position. 2Sheds braced himself for action but Joram spoke again, "What do you want from us? We do not want any trouble."

Grey Bob answered "We want to leave this person with you for a few days. We are climbing the big mountain to the north of you and do not want to take him with us."

"That will be fine but he cannot stay in that cage. It is too small."

"Put him somewhere bigger but do not lose him. We must go now."

Just then Piper and Calico reached the top of the stairs. 2Sheds whispered to her what was going on and she immediately flipped and started to push forward venting her fury.

Without a second thought, 2Sheds grabbed her arm and pulled her into the

kitchen. He pressed her against the wall and held his hand over her mouth.
"Shut up, Joram has this sorted and will let the boy out as soon as they are gone."
Piper was now spitting feathers of rage but he didn't let her go. Within minutes they could hear the soldiers going back down the stairs. He then dropped his hold on her and the two lovers faced each other with anger in their eyes.

    Piper and Calico raced onto the roof as Joram and Obie were cutting the string that kept the cage together. As the top came off, Piper bent down and lifted Maximus into the air. His legs remained crossed. She sat down with him on a chair.
"I can't feel my legs," he cried."What have they done to me ?"
"Let's take him down to the springs and let him soak in the warm water," said Joram. "That should help."

He carefully lifted the small boy into his arms and hurried off. Rafi and Calico followed.

2Sheds returned to the kitchen and Piper stood dazed by her own actions. How she wished she could have handled her feelings differently. This time she thought she had overreacted and 2Sheds had been justified in pulling her away. She thought he would not accept her apology so presumed that her only course of action was to carry on as normal. She felt sick for messing this up especially for her family who loved him dearly.

Cooking the meal together became terribly uncomfortable. She informed 2Sheds that Frank was coming to the meal but he did not reply, just carried on making the vegetarian roast.

Joram brought a sleepy Maximus back, wrapped in a towel. His legs were outstretched and did not feel numb anymore.

"He has had a drink and eaten some chocolate so I'll put him on one of the children's beds to have a sleep. Hopefully he will be brighter when he wakes up." Frank had time to check on Maximus before the roast dinner. He was appalled to find out about Grey Bob and her threadbare soldiers and would inform the security guards who were patrolling the area.

Obie took this opportunity to reveal his latest findings from the journals. Balbina and Cassia had written of the blue veined men who had pillaged Gratitude and taken away many of their young people.
Florin wrote about the aftermath of this barbaric and inhuman attack on a peace loving people.

"Some fathers banded together to go and find their sons and daughters but they never returned. Remaining families fled to the mountains and did not come back. It was not long before the palace was abandoned leaving its art as a reminder of a better time."

Other write-ups were similar, personal eye witness accounts of the power of evil. Atticus was the last person to write in the journal. He was an old man now and still grieved for his lost life.

"The beautiful Gracious Angels are now scattered throughout the land. They are still sought after because of their extraordinary ability to make things and because they are different. God wanted us to show the path to harmony and equality but evil men have sought to destroy us. They have taken over much of this land and their greed and selfishness knows no bounds. The atrocities they have carried out have no words to describe them.
God help us !

Obie stopped reading his translation and said, "Possibly God heard the prayer of Atticus because this land was annihilated and all that was left were very deep grey particles. But how that happened nobody knows.

Piper sat up straight in her chair, "I think I know why these people were different. I am sure that my friend Gogo was one of their descendants. She spent her early years as a feral animal, probably brought up by cats and was discovered in early adolescence sleeping in a car that she was repairing. Nobody had shown her what she had to do.. She just knew what needed to be done."

Piper stopped talking to have a drink of water. She continued,
"When I met her, Gogo did not know if she was a boy or a girl. With respect to her, I will keep the details private but my point in telling you is that I suspect this might have been something that others in her race shared. There were no gender issues with the Gracious Angels, just equality with a shared worth and value of the individual."

"And possibly physical characteristics that would appeal to the warped minds of the blue veined men," added 2Sheds, realisation finally dawning on him. What was it Piper had said to him on her first night back from Greysands. Something about an operation!!!

Chapter 16

The next day had been planned as a trip to the lake for everyone. A picnic would be put together and they would come back later in the afternoon.

"I'm not sure we can go now," said Ivy. It's too far for Maximus to walk."
"Oh no," said Rafi, already in his wetsuit. 2Sheds looked up from his book,
"It's okay Raf, I'll stay here. I'd like to have a look at the journals and read the translation, if that's okay with you Obie.

"Yes of course, we seem to be putting together a clearer picture of the history of these people but still no idea of how it was all destroyed."

Piper was disappointed that he wasn't going with them but was pleased that they weren't arguing with each other. She had to just let it all blow over and remember next time to be a little less frantic.

The daytrippers set off with picnic food in their backpacks leaving Maximus exercising his legs by walking around the perimeter of the rooftop. There was a brick wall at the base of the mountain slope and he sometimes sat on it for a rest or stepped on top of it to push his recovery. He seemed to find it within his capabilities and jumped back down with ease.

Maximus had shown no signs of wanting to run away and seemed to interact well with everyone. He looked reassured when he was told that they would protect him against Grey Bob and her men.

2Sheds pulled a small table near the large glass doors and he told Maximus to shout if he needed anything. Calico and Rafi had shown him how to play Super Mario the night before and he could play that if he wanted.

2Sheds then settled himself down to read the manuals and hoped to find some answers to his concerns. He looked up a couple of times to see the boy with his hands in the surface soil at the far end of the roof. Here there seemed to be a long, narrow opening in the sandstone.
A protruding mound stuck out from what appeared to be the base of the fissure. Below it, the rock remained joined.

Perhaps he is looking for fossils thought 2Sheds, as he returned to his reading. After a while, he could hear a kind of rumbling noise . He went on reading. Then he heard a dragging noise. He looked up to see that Maximus had pulled a length of rope out of a hole in the surface of the mountain. The rope had a handle at one end and was attached to a long piece of wood which in turn had rungs sticking out at regular intervals.

The more the boy pulled, the more the rungs stuck out like footholds and then 2Sheds realised that Maximus was escaping up the mountain.
"Maximus stop," shouted 2Sheds but it was too late. On hearing his voice, the boy dropped the rope, jumped onto the wall and, running up the footholds, disappeared behind the boulder.

2Sheds saw that the rope was disappearing back into the hole and the footholds were being drawn back in. He quickly grabbed the handle and started to pull and made sure that the wood rungs were fully extended before he let go and ran to the top. Just in time, he grabbed the top of the boulder as the steps slipped back into the surface soil with some of it sliding down and spilling onto the roof.

Piper and the others would have a hard time working out what had happened but he had to keep going. Still holding onto the top of the boulder he walked sideways around it to see that the long, narrow crack extended right through to an unknown exit about one hundred metres away.

There was no sign of Maximus. This route was going to be tricky for 2Sheds because it was not wide enough for him to put one foot in front of the other.

First he tried stepping his left foot forward and then sliding his right to join it. This became tedious so he planted his two hands on one side and two feet on the other and in a sort of giant turtle shape tried to move along sideways. This became more tedious so using a mixture of the two methods he arrived at the end and falling over his own feet fell out into a scene from The Sound of Music.

The hills weren't alive with music but they were lush in misty green vegetation. As he looked in front of him, he saw acres of forest sloping gently down the mountain. There was no sign of Maximus. He looked to the right and saw an extension of green landscape but when he looked in the opposite direction, he could see a flat wedge of land that was slightly different from the rest of the landscape.

In the midst of a mountain rainforest on the slopes of the mountain, walls, terraces and steps blended seamlessly into its natural setting. Stonework dwellings formed two terraces facing each other. Terraced gardens with stone walls were built further down the slope with a bigger building, possibly a place of worship below them.

He decided to look there first and ran over to the stone steps that would take him up to the top terrace of houses. They were old and most of the roofs had long gone but a couple had new wooden ones. That was a hopeful sign. He was nearly at the top when he heard a noise like a car horn. He stopped and nothing happened. The car horn noise honked again and there was the sound of feet running down towards it. There were also voices shouting to each other. 2Sheds turned and ran back down and ran across the grass to see a group of Maximus look-a-likes trying to get into a car.

    But it was not just any car. It was Gogo's car and even had the same trailer fixed to it. 2Sheds kept on running and shouting and waving his arms. Gogo had been revving the engine but stopped when she heard him shouting and got out of the car. She recognised 2Sheds and whooped and hollered as she ran towards him. They hugged each other and 2Sheds swung her around.

"WOW, WOW, WOW," laughed Gogo. "We meet again, my friend. Jump in, we're off to do battle with some unwelcome guests."

"Not Grey Bob and her merry men ?" he laughed.

Once everyone was settled and the car and trailer were overflowing with Grey Angels of all ages, they drove away.

The roof window was open and some of the gang were standing up singing battle songs at the tops of their voices.

"You do know that these guys have rifles with ammunition? asked 2Sheds having had a moment to think over what was happening.

" We most certainly do but we have a plan and you guys back there remember when I give the word, stop singing and crouch down."

"Ok, what's the plan?" asked 2Sheds, ready to be impressed.

" Run them over and stop their brutality once and for all ?" said Gogo cheerfully. "Oh, there's old hook nose now. She's coming around that clump of trees. Right everyone, be quiet and hunker down. We'll wait until we can see them all."

She stopped the car and sat up straight.

"I don't think I can be a part of this Gogo. I'll get out here."

Gogo began to laugh, "Sheds ! You do know that these wretched creatures are robots. They are A1s that went AWOL a very long time ago."

"Are you absolutely sure of this ?"
"Too late now," she declared as she started the car and proceeded towards the whole battalion walking single file up the mountain. They had not been programmed about motor vehicles and just kept walking into the path of the car with no change of expression on their faces.

Now 2Sheds knew why Gogo had a bull bar at the front of her car. She ploughed through the soldiers without stopping. He immediately closed his eyes as the kids in the back whooped and cheered on the destruction of the rogue soldiers.

"I didn't think we would see any blood," said Gogo seriously.

"What do you mean, blood ?" shouted 2Sheds before he heard the angels laughing and knew he had been tricked.

After a lot of bumping and squashing the car stopped.

" Right guys, can you dig me a hole to put the remains in?" asked Gogo.

Nobody answered but they all jumped out, picked up spades from the trailer and started work.

2Sheds eventually opened his eyes and got out of the car to view the carnage. Gogo was right the soldiers were not human but just to freak him out just that little bit more; of all the heads in all the world,

Grey Bob's head rolled down the slope and landed at his feet !!

It took the angels an hour to dig the hole, collect the body parts and fill it back in afterwards. They were hard working and thorough, even cleaning off the spades afterwards. 2Sheds declined the offer to keep the head of Grey Bob as a souvenir. He wasn't going to live down
his misunderstanding that easily.

Soon they were back in the car and cruising down the mountain. Gogo still had her Beatles cd and everyone was singing along to the songs,

"I'll give you all I've got to give,
  If you say you love me too,
  I may not have a lot to give
  But what I've got I'll give to you.
  I don't care to much for money
  For money can't buy me love……."

At the bottom of the mountain they came across an open space in the forest.

The atmosphere was dryer here and a river ran close by.
"A beautiful forest glade. Just perfect," sighed Gogo.
Who wants to camp here?"
"Yeahhhhh......" was the response from the lads and lasses in the back.
Gogo stopped and everyone tumbled out.
"I'll catch some fish for supper," shouted one youngster.
"I'll look for firewood," said another.
"I'll fix up some shelter," and soon they were all busily involved in setting up camp. Gogo and 2Sheds remained sitting in the car.
"They're great kids," said Gogo, noticing her friend's impressed expression. "Many of them have lived solitary lives until I started searching for them.
2Sheds was watching Maximus making a fire with twigs and branches on the banks of the river. In no time, he had made sparks and set the kindling alight.

"Is that what you do? asked 2Sheds to Gogo.
"Yes it is and I'm not going to stop until I find them all. It's my mission."
  Maximus was passed a kettle to heat water in. Already several fish had been caught in a net.
"And Gratitude Palace is waiting for them." added 2Sheds, feeling good that this story would have a great ending.
"Will you drive over and meet Piper and Calico? They will be so happy to see you."
"Hang on, are you saying they are in the group staying there? Maximus says the place is well guarded. He doesn't think we will get it back from your people."
    2Sheds turned towards Gogo,
 "The archaeologists and construction workers have been working there for a long time. They have tried to reconstruct the site to its original glory. They have found journals and attempted to piece together the history of Gratitude but it is most

definitely for your people. There is no doubt about that. "

"But why are you there ?" Gogo was flabbergasted. This was news to her.

"John helped with the restoration of the site. A lot of our skilled workers from Abednego were here. When it was finished and before a search began for the indigenious people like yourselves, he invited a small group of us to meet up for a get together.

"We had no idea this was happening for us" gasped Gogo." It's a good job that you chased after Maximus or we would have shied away from you all,"

One of the angels had gutted the fish and Maximus had started to cook them. Meanwhile a shelter had been constructed with branches tied together and large rainforest leaves covering the frame.

2Sheds continued, "We never did get together because John was invited into Heaven for a celestial meeting. He is still planning to meet us at the palace when he returns."

"What revelations ! It's amazing news. I guess we had better go and help the youngsters. It looks like we are staying here tonight so we can share the news over our meal and start out for the palace early tomorrow".

Chapter 17

The fish supper was cooked to perfection. Someone had found wild spinach and potatoes and everyone had their fill. 2Sheds thought it was one of the most enjoyable meals he had ever tasted. Whatever was in the river water was extremely refreshing and put everyone in a very chilled mood.

When the meal was over and they all sat chatting around the fire that Maximus had made. Gogo told them about Gratitude

Palace and that it was ready for them to move in. There was great emotion with some youngsters linking arms and dancing. Some of them cried to think they were going to live in the home of their ancestors. They were no longer homeless.

Eventually they all sat back down and chatted amongst themselves. 2Sheds told Gogo about his relationship with Piper and how they were becoming a family unit. She in turn told him about her partner. She was called Valentina and was a fellow gracious angel.

When Gogo, Calico and Patch passed through the entrance into Heaven, they danced for joy with their feet rarely touching the soft grass. Gogo had waved goodbye to Piper and Stanley and waltzed off into a glorious sunset.

Calico and Patch had a sudden change of mind and in fear of losing Piper and Stanley, turned back in tears and raced back to them. Gogo carried on and felt hysterically happy as tears ran down her face. She didn't know where she was going but knew it was the right thing to do. Eventually the path she was following led to an opening and she saw a semi circle of stone houses in front of her. The stones were specifically cut to fit together and were very similar to the ones she would see at the abandoned site behind Gratitude Palace.

    This site wasn't abandoned and looked vibrant and busy. People with dreadlocks and beautiful faces were coming to meet her. They were waving and bringing her flowers. When they met, a beautiful Gracious Angel stepped closer and gave Gogo a heavenly bunch of flowers. She said that she was Gogo's grandmother and embraced her.

    A feast of perfect fruit was laid out with a selection of desserts and cakes. Everyone made her feel welcome. She was told that her parents were living in exile but their whereabouts was unknown. This seemed the fate for most of the descendants of the angels that had survived the destruction of their land.

This was when Gogo first met Valentina. She drove up in the most unusual car. It was long and sleek with an open top. It was baby blue in colour and looked like it had wings. When she swung her long legs out of the car, Gogo could see that she was wearing a white tunic over black trousers with a short black waistcoat. Valentina had jet black dreads with the front ones greased back giving her the cool look Elvis Presley would make his trademark in the Earth World.

As well as Valentina, there were five or six young dreadsters, who jumped out of the car and were immediately embraced by their ancestors. They looked unkempt and malnourished.

Gogo was fascinated by Valentina and could not take her eyes off her. She even momentarily forgot how to speak when Valentina came up to introduce herself,
"I hear you can drive," she said. "Perhaps you might be interested in helping me search out these poor forgotten little dreadsters."

At that moment the little dreadsters were busy stuffing their faces with food and drink while Gogo was trying to remember how to speak,
"Okay," was all she managed.
"Okay it is then," laughed Valentina. "Jump in and let's go."
"But I've only just arrived. People might be offended if I leave so quickly."
"Don't be daft. This is eternity, we have all of time to be together but many of our exiled family are still hungry and homeless."

Sounding the horn on her car, Valentina and Gogo waved goodbye and drove away.

"Where are we going?" asked Gogo, feeling a great sense of freedom as Valentina pressed a button to retract
the roof.
"Shall we go and pick up your car?
We can tow it back and add some improvements to it."
"But I left it back in Greysands," exclaimed Gogo.
"By a high ridge of pebbles. I know, it needs to be moved."
"Have you been there?" Gogo was incredulous.
"I saw aerial footage of it. Taken by a drone that was sent in to investigate," answered Valentina.
"So how will we get there?"
"I know a shortcut. Straight from heaven to hell you could say," laughed Valentina.
    Gogo stopped talking to admire the beautiful scenery whizzing past.
They were in grasslands so perfectly wonderful, it took her breath away.

She had already spied a pride of lions stretched out in the sun and a pack of prairie dogs off on a jaunt. Beautiful birds could be seen taking a lift on the backs of bison. It was a paradise of health and beauty with nothing for anyone to fear. After many miles the environment began to change and became slightly mountainous and Valentina took the turning into a canyon with a steady flow of water running down the middle. The sides were steep on both sides and Valentina raised the roof.

"Soon we turn off for Greysands and then it will be decidedly nicer under cover. We need to look out for a division in the road where we have to choose the one that will be full of dense air and very uninviting."
"I did not think I would ever be going back," replied Gogo.
"It won't be for long and it will be worth it to get your car back."
Valentina suddenly stopped the car. Gogo had not even noticed that the road

branched off to the left. She had mistaken it for a continuation of the rock but of a different colour. Looking closer, the atmosphere in the new road was a thick wet substance.

"I don't fancy this." said Valentina as she turned down the road but she could not move the car through this thick gooey substance.

"Let's reverse back to that red line across the road and have a think." suggested Gogo. Valentina reversed back to the line in the road and turned the engine off. The two women were at a loss to know what to do.

"Perhaps we continue on the other road and see if there is another left turn," suggested Gogo.

As they were mulling this over, a scratched red van came zooming out of nowhere and nearly drove straight into them. The driver immediately started blowing his horn for them to move.

"I'll go and ask him what he plans to do?" Valentina got out and walked back to the van whereupon a small ragged little man got out. Standing in front of her, he came up to her chest and he was obviously very impatient. Gogo could see him raising his arms and gesturing wildly. Eventually Valentina returned smiling.

"Apparently I'm doing it all wrong and if I reverse back, he will show us the way."

The two vehicles reversed further back until the red van had room to overtake and plant his front wheels directly on the red line. He was most specific about that, even getting out of the van to check his position.

Within minutes, some sort of whirling dervish started to revolve around the entrance, causing the goo to be spun around and discharged in all directions. It seemed to be thinning as it moved around.

The man revved his engine and drove into the mass and Valentina followed behind. It was like driving through lumpy porridge. Large globules slid down the windscreen and took no notice of the windscreen wipers. Luckily this did not take long and within seconds they were through this nauseous plug and onto the barren world of Greysands.

The red van was driving straight on and the girls decided to follow him for want of a better idea. At least he seemed to know where he was going. After miles of monotonous greyness from the sky to the ground, Gogo noticed a chink of light to her left,

"Let's check that out,"

Valentina changed direction and headed towards the light. Several palm trees and bushes became visible,

"It appears to be an oasis."

"Let's hope it is the one I came across when I was driving back from my mission to find an escape route out of here." said Gogo hopefully.

"If it is, will you know which way we should go to find the car?"

"I will definitely be able to find the white house and that will take us to the coastline."

As luck would have it, Gogo was certain that the waterhole was the one that she had visited. On that occasion, she had driven her car under three palm trees growing in a triangular shape and hid from Tanic Clay's helicopter flying overhead.

Valentina drove her car into the same spot and immediately Gogo knew the way to her original route. She could direct Valentina to the pebble ridge to find the car or they could visit the white house to take a break after the tedious journey.

Valentina jumped at the chance of a break and so they reached the house that evening. It looked dark and foreboding but Gogo knew where to find candles and wood to build a fire. There was plenty of tinned food fit to eat and Valentina had come with plenty of fresh food from the Gracious Angel's welcoming party.

The two women stayed in the house for five days and became friends, lovers and soul mates. They continually heated the boiler with coal and had constant hot water. They would bathe together in the big tub before melting into each other on the multilayer bed they made in the lounge in front of the large fireplace. They dined on tinned vegetables and noodles followed by fruit with evaporated milk.

They would talk and discuss everything and anything. They eagerly listened to each other and relished each other's ideas and explanations. It was during this time that they both committed to searching and finding every Gracious Angel and bringing them home.

On the fifth day, they tidied up and set off to pick up Gogo's car. She had not seen it since the evening that John Bartlebee and 2Sheds had rescued her and her friends. The two men had arrived on the beach in a hovercraft and taken them all to safety.

The abandoned car started immediately and still had plenty of petrol in the tank.

"I think it's an old London taxi. We should be able to restore it to its original condition and add an optional middle section for more passengers."

"Sounds good."

Valentina followed Gogo and they retraced their tracks back to the home of the Gracious Angels on the outskirts of Heaven. Gogo moved in with Valentina and they spent their days making a middle section for the old London taxi. The frame was made of narrow sections that concertinaed back into themselves. When opened, a vertical partition folded down to make a firm base and the side chairs could be swung forward. A row of folded chairs at the back then opened up to make more seating.

Gogo loved all the improvements to her car. They would now be able to rescue more dreadies in one trip. As soon as it was finished, Valentina and Gogo were on the road searching out their fellow angels. Sometimes they travelled together and sometimes separately.

When 2Sheds met up with Gogo, she was on a solo mission with the plan to meet up with Valentina a few days down the road. His revelations about the newly restored Gratitude Palace would now change everything.

Chapter 18

Back at Gratitude Palace, everyone was shocked by the sudden disappearance of 2Sheds and Maximus. There was no sign of any disturbance. Everything seemed just as they had left it. The only thing different was a layer of rubble on the roof beside the steep mountain edge. Surely that couldn't have anything to do with it!

Calico and Rafi searched every room calling out for 2Sheds. Piper asked Stanley to find him and he sniffed and barked at the rubble but that didn't help.. Obie and Ivy went to find Frank to find out if he had any news. Joram looked for tracks outside and Marigold and Maya thought they had better start preparing the evening meal.

When the night rolled in, everyone felt uneasy but tried to keep positive. Perhaps Maximus had done a runner and 2Sheds had gone after him. They were probably on their way back as they spoke. Inwardly Piper felt wretched especially because she regretted her outburst over freeing Max from the cage. She had let herself down in 2Shed's opinion and now he was gone and she might never be able to right the wrong.

Eventually everyone fell asleep hoping a new day would bring good news but this did not happen. In the morning, Joram went off to check for any updates from Frank. The day stretched before them and they had no idea what to do next. Obie suggested taking the donkey carts out and he and Ivy took one and Mia and Marigold took the other.

   Left to her own devices, Piper aimlessly brushed the floor upstairs when she suddenly heard Calico shouting that a big car was coming. Piper dropped the brush, plonked herself down on a cushion and slid down the slide. She was outside in no time and recognised Gogo's car driving into the courtyard. Horns were beeping, bells were ringing and multiple arms waving out of every window.

  2Sheds was taken by how lovely Piper looked as she stood at the top of the steps. All his previous anger evaporated and he just wanted to hold her in his arms again. The car stopped and he jumped out of the car at the same time as Gogo.
He stood and watched Piper run towards the car, thinking she was running to him but

he hadn't accounted for Gogo streaking past and straight into his girlfriend's arms.

    The girls clung to each other and jumped up and down on the spot. What joy was shared in that long awaited reunion. Calico clung to Gogo's legs and was picked up and Rafi threw his arms around Piper's waist and was not going to be left out of the celebrations. The dreadies tumbled out of the car willy nilly and were in awe of the sandstone palace in front of them.

    The only one who greeted 2Sheds was Stanley and he wasn't abandoning him even when the jubilant youngsters lifted the two women onto their shoulders and headed for the palace steps. It was only then that Piper looked around to find him and blew him a kiss. Ah well, he would have to be satisfied with that.

    Once inside, the dreadies lowered Gogo and Piper onto the ground and hurried off to explore. There was great excitement all around with Patch leaving his donkey mates to say hello to the person who had rescued him when he was only a few days old.

Upstairs Gogo was reunited with Obie, Ivy and Marigold and introduced to Joram and Maya. It was here that Piper and 2Sheds came together and he told her of his bizarre adventure.

During this time the dreadies had well and truly settled in. The ovens were lit and food was being prepared. Maximus knew where there were more tents and sleeping bags and they were being set up in every free space. A few of them had even started painting and sculpting. The palace rang out with the happy sound of contentment and joy. The Gracious Angels had come home.

The evening meal was pure perfection with the youngsters producing a variety of dishes from vegetable curries to lentil roasts. It turned out that Maximus also knew where to find the wine cellar and the meal turned into a grand feast.

Afterwards as everyone sat around the firepit, 2Sheds told everyone about following the young boy up the mountain and finding Gogo on the other side. She in turn took over to tell the story of him thinking Greybob was human and his horror of running her over. 2Sheds could tell that his friends had thought the same as him as they sort of laughed at his reaction.

"Do you mean that Greybob was really Greybot?" said Calico. "I didn't know that." As usual her young brain had simply summed up the situation.

As she sat warming herself by the fire, Piper was looking for closure, "Since we have been here we have chatted to the archaeologist and read several historical accounts but we still don't know what actually happened to destroy this land?" asked Piper. "Do you know Gogo?"

"I will tell you what I know and what I have always known but I don't know how I know it," she laughed. "If that makes any sense."

Everyone seemed to have stopped what they were doing and were listening to her now.

"Is Max here?" she asked.

The boy stood up.

"We've only known you a short while Max and in that time has anyone talked to you about the destruction of Greysands?"

"No, there's not really been a lot of time for talking.but I will ask someone if you want me too," answered the young boy.

"No, that's fine," she said reassuringly. "Because I want you to tell us what you believe happened to this land. I think that we angels will all tell the same story. It's the essence of God that is inside all of us. We were born with this knowledge in our souls."

The boy looked worried.

Gogo said "Would you tell us in your own words, the answer to Piper's question?

"All I know is a story that God was visiting this land because a lot of very bad things were happening here. He came across an old lady dying on her veranda. All her animals lay dead or dying around her. He saw her hands lying on her lap and a gaping hole was where her ring finger used to be. He picked her up and summoned his angels to carry her to Heaven with all her animals.

When they had gone, he stamped his feet four times on the ground causing an enormous earthquake. God thrust his arms into the air and the whole of Graysands rose up. Every living creature, every living tree and plant was gone. Everything man had built was also gone……..

Gogo raised her hand and smiled, "That's great Max, shall I finish the story for you?,"

" Yes please," he said, glad to be out of the limelight.

" For three days the contents of Greysands hurtled higher and higher into the atmosphere. On the fourth day it stopped and returned to the ground but not whole as it was before. It poured down as tiny grey particles that covered the whole land to a depth of twenty feet."

Gogo had finished the story and a round of applause and murmurs of approval rose from the audience.

"This is the story we have in our hearts," said Gogo.

Chapter 19

The super efficient angels quickly took over all the basic tasks needed to be done which left the group of friends with little to do. They still had not heard from John and presumed it would be any day that he came to see them.

After that, Obie and Ivy would return to Abednego and make plans for their return to The Earth World and Joram,

Maya and Marigold would go back to Juniper Island. This left Piper and 2Sheds to spend time with John and mull over his news, whatever it would be.

Not having daily tasks was pleasant but when a group chat with John was shared by all, it was a sign for them to move on. John was sitting in his comfy chair in his den on Abednego. Tom Cat was happily curled up on his lap.

John looked relaxed. He said that he had returned a few days before but had needed time to think over his experiences.

"I hope nobody minds if I don't fly over but I'm here if you need me."

"I need you," said Calico. "It's been ages since I saw you!"

"Well, it won't be long and we can video chat every day now that I'm back," he replied fondly.

Stanley's tail was wagging at the sound of John's voice.

"Hi John, remember me?" broke in Gogo.

"Of course I do. You look great. More like a Goldie than a Gogo now."
Gogo laughed, "And that's what my beautiful girlfriend calls me."
"I'm going to call you Goldie too," added Calico.
The video chat continued with everyone having a chance to speak. Even Patch brayed hello.

It was decided that the friends would fly back to Abednego in two days' time. They would travel in the same plane that they had arrived in. Gogo looked anxious, "Valentina will be picking up some of our grey angels from Heaven and bringing them here to continue their mortal lives in Gratitude. I do hope she meets you and 2Sheds before you go." said Gogo to Piper.
"I hope so too." she replied.
As it turned out, Valentina would not be arriving until the afternoon of the day that the others would have already left by plane.

Gogo and Piper were disappointed.

"I know what we can do," suggested 2Sheds.

"Me, Piper and Stan can fly back in the helicopter on the following day."

"That's brilliant," responded Gogo looking relieved.

"I have told her so much about you both. It will be wonderful to have you all together." Piper put her arm around Gogo's shoulders, "And hopefully we can meet up on a regular basis from now on."

On the morning that the plane was ready for flight, there seemed a wistful sadness amongst everyone. The holiday was over and the group was aware that two of them would not be returning. What they did not know then, was that several of them would not be coming back. This was the end of a collective experience where a lot of life lessons were learnt from the present and the past.

Lessons that would help them in their journey through life.

Calico was sad to leave Piper but was persuaded to go when she was told that she would be having a sleepover in John's den.

"With Rafi and Patch ?" she asked as Piper was edging her towards the plane.

"Of course !" said Rafi. He took her hand and led her up the steps. He was turning into a no nonsense boy and that was appreciated by Piper.

Gracious Palace seemed reborn. Since the young Gracious Angels had arrived (not Grey Angels or dreadies anymore) the whole place had come alive. Paintings were displayed on every wall and statues placed in every corner. Maximus' knowledge of the palace almost doubled the volume of its contents.

A library of books was uncovered and adjoining caves full of tools and art materials. It was a wondrous treasure trove for the angels to revive their inheritance.

    Valentina arrived late in the afternoon. Her baby blue Cadillac Convertible was a wonder to behold and was enveloped in angels before she even had time to stop. The car was already piled high with expectant newcomers who were waving coloured streamers at their comrades.

    When Valentina managed to get through the joyous mob, she saw Gogo at the top of the steps. She started to walk towards her and the angels all stepped back like the parting of The Red Sea and she had a clear pathway. They formed the waves on either side and whooped and waved their streamers. Valentina and Gogo fell into each other's arms.

    The celebrations followed the couple up the inner steps and into the middle room where they stood and clapped their heroes into the palace. After a few minutes, they stopped, turned and flowed back down the steps.

Left alone, Valentina and Gogo shared a few moments together before Gogo called 2Sheds and Piper into the room, "Guys I am so happy to introduce you to Valentina. It's great to have you all here in one place. We just need Amalie or I should say Mary Lee to complete the party."

"Well I'm sure that won't be long in happening now that we know where to find you." said Piper as she approached the couple. She held out her hand to Valentina who held it and pulled her in close for a hug. She also pulled 2Sheds into the same embrace.

"I'm going to show Valentina where to drop her bags and then show her around her new home," said Gogo excitedly. "Shall we meet you in the springs later?"

"Good idea, I'm going to take Stanley for a walk first," chipped in Piper.

"And I had better check out the helicopter. It hasn't been used for a while," added 2Sheds.

He thought this was going to be uneventful as he walked away from the palace. The helicopter had been kept at the archaeology site and was close to all the vehicles and tools needed for the dig.

As he got closer, he realised that it was not the same one that he had left there. It was obviously new, bigger and a more advanced model. He sat inside and checked out the new controls. It seemed to be a plush version of its predecessor and was extremely comfortable. A box lay on the passenger seat with a manual on top. Attached to it was an official note to say that the Lysie Fields Ministry of Flight had recalled the old helicopter and issued a replacement.

Fair enough thought 2Sheds as he opened the box. Inside were two tasers and a set of handcuffs. "
Bloody hell, is this a sign of trouble ahead?"

Chapter 20

Saying goodbye to everyone at Gracious Palace was emotional. Discovering the fate of Gratitude had been a humbling experience. These people had their beautiful life ripped away from them by vile and depraved human beings whose behaviour was beyond the laws of mankind. Many years of suffering had taken place until now and Piper and 2Sheds had found it uplifting to experience the reunion of The Gracious Angels as they regained their homeland and regained their birthright to be free.

Sitting together in the comfort of the brand new automatic helicopter, the two young people were quiet in contemplation of what they had experienced. Unlike Stanley who was stretched out on the back seat enjoying a very comfortable sleep. It was 2Sheds that broke the silence.

"Have you any concerns about John's news?" he asked as he gazed out at the endless monotony of Greysands around them.

"He did say that there was nothing to worry about so I guess we're going to be fine. Shall we go back to Rainbow Bridge?"

"Yey, that's a good idea. A good place for us to grow family roots," smiled 2Sheds. Piper stretched her legs in the spacious footwell and looked down to see what she had just kicked.

"What's in the box?" she asked, picking it up and putting it on her knee.

"You're not going to believe this. It's a taser gun and handcuffs. They must be issued with all the new choppers."

Piper opened the box and took out the gun.

"Just be careful. I don't fancy being totally incapacitated at the moment."

Piper laughed, "I'll be careful."

"Now why doesn't that reassure me."

"It's completely safe because I haven't put the cartridge in yet."

"Don't you dare !"

"Actually in this advanced model, you can use three cartridges for multiple shots before having to reload," she teased.

Piper carefully put the gun back in the box but took out the manual to read.

"Did you know that every muscle in your body locks up after a hit?" said 2Sheds.

" Yes, and it lasts at least five seconds. I read somewhere that grown men have screamed with the pain and have not been able to move at all. Just thinking is pretty difficult at such times."

Piper looked up to see that they were leaving Greysands and flying straight through into the Earth World. "I didn't expect that. I thought we would fly through The Lysie Fields first."
"So did I but maybe this is a shortcut."
"It shouldn't be long now," said Piper, putting the manual back in the box and replacing it in the footwell.

The sun was setting on Earth and the mixture of glorious colour lit up the sky. Suddenly the two youngsters felt a sense of coming home under this majestic sky. Two hours later they could see Abednego in the distance and it reminded Piper of the first time she had seen this wonderful ocean liner. She had been in a helicopter on that occasion too but not in the good health she was today. She had a serious head injury caused by her bully of a stepfather pushing her down a flight of concrete steps.

It was getting dark now and the ship with its tall black funnels was enveloped in a myriad of tiny lights. As they drew closer to the top deck, they could see John waving to them. He seemed to be carrying something long and padded over one arm and waving with the other. He had a large bag used for rescues at his feet.
"Don't say we're on duty already," said 2Sheds jokingly.
"I shouldn't have thought so," replied Piper, waving back to John.
"Stan, wake up. I can see John."
Stanley's ears pricked up. He sat up and looked out the side window until he could see John. Then it was a matter of standing up, wagging his tail and raring to get out.

The helicopter touched down and Piper and Stan tumbled out of the door to see him. Piper thought how special John looked, almost hallowed. He hugged them both for a long moment and then did the same to 2Sheds.

"It seems a long time since I last saw you. So much has happened in between times."

"Especially for you," added Piper.

"It sure has and the truth be told, I'm finding it hard to adjust."

"Will you be able to tell us stuff?" asked 2Sheds.

" Yes I will but first I have a favour to ask you."

"Hence the padded suits," grinned 2Sheds knowingly.

"Yep,I thought I had arranged a helicopter to pick up a little boy abandoned in a snowstorm. He is going to die of hypothermia if we don't get there within the hour.

"Okay, have you got the route?"

"It's already programmed into the helicopter's computer. I did remember to do that. You're going to a remote farm, miles from any towns. The complete journey,there and back, should not take more than a couple hours. We are already off the coast of Scotland now."

"Okay, we'll be off. I'm presuming Stanley will stay with you while we're gone," said Piper.

"It will be a pleasure. Come on Stan, let's find some supper."

"And what about the nitwits?" she asked.

"Safely tucked up in bed. Jack and Mary are with them. They have come over to see you all."

"I hoped they would," said Piper, with a big grin on her face.

"Has Cody come over with them?" asked 2Sheds.

"Apparently he wanted to stay for the tennis tournament. He's staying with Joram and Maya's parents."

"That's great. It's a game he seems to enjoy.

Okay, we'd better get going," said 2Sheds as he took the thermal suits from John. Piper picked up the two pairs of snow boots

and put them on the back seat of the helicopter.
She then came back for the first aid bag.
"There's a thermal suit to put the lad in as soon as you can and some small bottles he should be able to drink unaided.
Just pull off the strip for the milk to warm to the right temperature."
"Okay boss, see you soon," and Piper kissed him on the cheek.

Chapter 21

The helicopter was up in the air in minutes and flying through the night sky. It was enveloped in darkness with only its own lights shining ahead.
Piper was holding the snow suits that 2Sheds had passed over to her.
"I bet the nitwits were excited to see Gramps and Mary," said Piper.

"I'm sure they were. I still find it strange to call her Mary. I think I will always think of her as Amalie."

"I suppose it's easier for me because Gramps always told me stories about her when I was little. He was heartbroken to lose her."

"Do they know that we are an item now?"

"I don't know. Maybe if they have met up with Ivy and Obadiah," said Piper rather thoughtfully.

"Will they approve?" he teased.

"I don't knowww….!" she said, feeling uncomfortable with the question. "Anyway we're breaking through into The Earth World soon and here comes the snow. We need to concentrate."

Piper had not finished speaking before the windscreen was covered in snow. At first it was isolated snow flakes but within a few minutes they were inside an igloo. "Do we have wipers?" asked Piper.

"Of course." 2Sheds pressed a button and two elongated shaped arms moved their vertical blades from the mid section of each window to the outer rim. They were now flying over a snow covered landscape. "We had better get the gear on," said 2Sheds.

Piper passed over his suit. It was slightly tricky putting it on in a sitting down position but they managed. There was an inner padded layer to keep them warm.
"Good job the controls are all automatic," laughed Piper as she watched her boyfriend wriggling around to get his arms in the right hole.
"If not we'd probably end up stuck in a tree or swinging from the top of a telegraph pole," he agreed.

Piper passed over his snow boots and the youngsters finished their preparations apart from their headwear.
"Won't be long now Piper. The helicopter will be landing at the top of the

neighbouring field. The nearby gate will take us into a farmyard where three large sheds have been erected on the opposite side.

"How do you know all this?" asked Piper, looking puzzled.

"John is typing this up on my phone as I speak," 2Sheds' phone was in the phone holder on the helicopter dashboard.

"He says that we must turn left out of the gate and the farmhouse is about one hundred yards in front of us. The little boy has sheltered in a log bin near the front door."

I can't understand why nobody has found him," said Piper.

"They can't be looking for him I suppose," stated 2Sheds, vexed by the poor boy's appalling circumstances.

    The helicopter started to descend onto the snow laden ground and as soon as Piper felt the landing skids touch down, she put on the balaclava and pulled the hood over her head and fastened it securely. 2Sheds did the same before grabbing the treatment bag and jumping out and running to the gate. Piper was close behind him. They were surprised how deep the snow was.

They left the gate open for their return. The one thing that was strikingly obvious was the cacophony of dogs barking in the sheds. Some were desperate and constant. Some were menacing and vicious. Others were intermittent yelps. Piper found this most disturbing.

The three sheds were straight in front of them so they turned to see a stone built house at the top of some steps. A light was on in the room beside the porch but the curtains were closed. They clambered up the snow covered steps and came to the log bin. A sheet of tarpaulin covered the top and in one corner a small hand was visible. It was holding down the sheet.

2Sheds took off the tarpaulin and lifted out a small child. It was obvious at first sight that he was inadequately dressed for the ice and snow. 2Sheds held him against his body as Piper held the thermal suit ready to put it on him. She had already put some of the milk bottles from the bag into her pocket. She whipped off his wellington boots and put his legs into footed trousers as she pulled the rest of the suit up onto his back. She then quickly put his arms in the gloved arms of the jacket and 2Sheds turned him around. Piper pulled on the hood and zipped him securely in the coverall thermal suit.

"Is he still breathing?" she asked.

"I think so. Have you got the milk?"

Piper took a small chunky bottle from her pocket and removed the tag to warm the milk inside. By the time she passed the milk over to 2Sheds it would be at the correct temperature. He cradled the boy in one arm as he gently pushed the teat into his mouth.

"Let's go," said 2Sheds.

Piper turned to pick up the treatment bag and as she did, noticed a gap in the curtained window. She took a closer look through and froze from the sight in front of her. The freezing did not have anything to do with the extreme weather conditions but of a man that she had thought she would never see again. He was pouring himself a glass of whiskey. Piper's blood ran cold.

Without warning, she heard a forceful whistle and visibly jumped. It was 2Sheds down by the gate. With her mind in turmoil she ran after him. By the time she reached the helicopter, 2Sheds had the pilot's door open with the front seat pushed forward. He was gently propping the boy onto the back seat and strapping him in. His face was already looking a better colour as he suckled the warm milk and honey.

"What are you doing ?" shouted 2Sheds when he heard her turning out the bag.

"Just getting some bottles of milk." She carried on as he pushed his seat back, sat down and shut his door.

This was her chance. She placed the bottles on the seat, shut her door and ran around to his side of the helicopter.

2Sheds hadn't noticed and had started the engine. He looked up confused, "What are you doing?"

"I'm not coming with you."

"Don't be so bloody stupid. Get in." he shouted.

"Ask John to send another pilot back for me,"

2Sheds started to get out.

"Don't, the boy needs help. Go"

The little lad was starting to cry and 2Sheds turned to see him.

Piper took the moment to run away carrying the treatment bag.

2Sheds was furious. He had no idea what was going on with Piper. He couldn't go after her because of the little boy's condition. He guessed it must be something to do with the plight of the dogs in the sheds. If only she wasn't so strong willed, they could easily have contacted the local emergency services to sort the situation out in the morning.

    Once up in the air, 2Sheds looked across at the passenger's seat and saw the bottles of milk. Why had she taken the treatment bag? It would be empty.
Then the truth dawned on him. He leant across and swept his hand over the floor of the footwell. The box containing the taser gun, cartridges and handcuffs was gone. Piper had taken them in the bag.

Chapter 22

Piper ran through the trodden snow in the footprints that were already made. She reached the gate and stopped. She could hear a man's voice calling out a name. At first she feared it was 2Sheds coming after her but it was a voice coming from in front of her not behind.

She slipped behind the tractor and crouched down out of sight. The voice was calling again and she was in no doubt now that it belonged to her nemesis, Victor Salomon. She saw him as he walked through the gate. He had a thick coat on now and high leather boots.
On his head he was wearing a trapper hat with fur lined ear flaps. Instantly a thought came into her head. Perhaps his ears were hypersensitive since she had tried to slice them off !!

Victor Salomon was calling for someone called Omar. Piper presumed that must be the name of the little boy they had rescued. Only Victor could be cruel enough to leave a young child to freeze to death. It would not have been the first time.

Within minutes the man with the sensitive ears was on his way back and he was not happy as he ranted random phrases to himself. His torch would highlight the mish mash of footprints as he made his way up the steps to the house but he was not looking for clues . He walked past the front door and the window and straight to the end of the front wall. Piper followed, only having the light from the gap in the curtains to guide her.

Victor turned down a path between the house and a large metal shed. Piper peeked around the corner and saw him unlocking the shed door and going inside. He was still ranting and it sounded like he was either throwing or kicking things out of his way. Piper edged forward, still trying to walk inside his footprints in the snow.

A light had been put on inside and through a dirty window, Piper could see a jumble of farming equipment and sacks. She could also see a large portacabin with curtained windows attached to the sides of the shed. A light was already on inside. Victor pulled back the bolts of a glass door and went inside. He was still shouting and now she could hear a woman crying hysterically.

Piper removed the key from the outer shed and very quietly went inside. She looked around at the equipment which seemed to be old and worn.
The woman sounded terribly upset and the poor dogs sounded louder than ever. It was mayhem. Piper wondered if she was the mother of the little boy in the log bin. If so, she would try to let her know what had

happened and help reunite them on Abednego.

After more ranting and raving in Arabic, Victor stormed out of the glass door but did not forget to bolt it securely. He strode over to the outer door and could not find the key. He searched his pockets and then the floor but had no success so he kicked the door and walked off. He was definitely a troubled man.

Piper waited a few minutes and then walked over to the glass door and unbolted it. She could hear the woman sobbing. Piper walked in to see that the woman was sitting at a dining table. The place was designed like a very basic one bedroom flat with all the basic requirements needed to survive. Everything looked second hand and shabby.

When the dark haired woman saw Piper, she jumped up in fright. Piper put her finger to her lips and walked forward. She just hoped that she could reassure her that she was there to help.

"Have you lost your little boy?" asked Piper kindly
"Have you seen him?" she begged.
"We have taken him to hospital. He was very cold and his body was shutting down.
The woman gasped "Will he be alright?"
"I don't know but I can take you to him when our helicopter comes back."
It's a good job that she can speak English, thought Piper.
"Victor won't let me go." she sobbed again. He is a bad man."
"I know, so we will have to escape but why is Victor so angry?"
 The woman dried her eyes on her sleeve and stood up, "He thinks you are police and will find out the bad things that happen here."
"Why are there so many dogs barking? Poor things sound very stressed."
"Victor has dogs for fighting and people come here to watch."
"Bloody hell, but why so many dogs?"

"Because he has a puppy farm too. I used to look after the pups with my sister but Victor made me pregnant and locked me away in here. He is horrible to my son and I think he has tried to kill him."

Piper could now see that the poor woman was heavily pregnant. She was wearing a thick jumper over a mid-length flannel dress and woollen tights. She had leather boots. Her hair was unruly and unwashed and tied back in a ponytail. She had smudged kohl pencil & mascara surrounding her brown eyes.

"What is your name?" asked Piper, keen to help and reassure her.
"Zara and my sister is Sofi. Victor won't let me see her."
Piper remembered that Victor could be back at any minute.
"Zara, go and put on some warm clothes and pick up anything you want to take with you. I will hide in the outer shed in case Victor comes back and locks us both in. Be quick".

Piper hurried outside and hid behind somes sacks of dried dog food. She was outraged at what was happening here and needed to get in touch with John as soon as she got back to the helicopter. She would have to check out the dogs and perhaps stay here even longer.

"I wish I'd cut his bloody head off," she said to the dismal shed.

Piper decided that this was a good time to load the taser gun. She took it out of her pocket with the box of cartridges and took three of them out. She thought that she might not get the chance to reload again. Luckily clicking in the cartridges was easy as they only fitted in one way. So hopefully she couldn't make a mistake.

Zara came out in an oversized duffle coat, woollen hat and gloves. She carried a zipped up cloth bag. Piper went to meet her at the cabin door. She shut and bolted it. The two women skirted along the side wall of the shed until they reached the outer door. Piper went ahead to check that nobody was outside. She beckoned Zara to follow her. They went outside and remembering that she had the key, Piper locked the door and kept the key. Anything that might hinder Victor was a worthwhile tactic.

Outside Zara directed Piper to the side of the shed that ran parallel to the first large barn. A snow covered bank of land separated the two buildings. Zara led Piper along the bank until they reached stone steps leading down. Now they had made fresh footprints but they had no choice. The noise of the barking dogs had lessened but it was the pitiful yelping that pierced Piper's heart. She had to do something to stop this.

Zara walked around the outside of the large wooden barn and nearly bumped into a man coming around the corner. He was tall and well wrapped up for the freezing conditions.

"Is that you Rashid? What are you doing out here?"

" Zara, we've been worried about you."

The man held her at arm's length to get a proper look at her.

"Salomon unlocked the shed and told us to hide in the woods. He said that police are here."

"Have you seen Sofi?" she asked anxiously.

"She stays in the kennels so maybe still locked in.

I have to go if police coming. Bye Zara."

And he was gone.

Zara turned to Piper. They could see each other by the light shining out of the building above them but it was dark and still very noisy.

"We are not supposed to be in this country. The police will send us back," blurted out Zara.

"Don't worry, we have helicopters to take you to our ship. Let's check out the kennels now. We might find Sofi."

When they walked to the front of the first building, they could see that both the double doors were wide open and lights were on inside. The interior seemed to be living quarters on the floor level and something clinical looking upstairs. There was a partition with glass windows closing off the top level. Piper thought it looked like a hospital with fluorescent lights shining down.
"What's going on up there?" asked Piper.
"Another bad thing." sighed Zara, looking around frantically for her sister. She hurried to the far end of the barn and came back.
"The people who were here worked with drugs upstairs. They mix chemicals with drugs to make more money.
"What chemicals?"
"Legal ones like mild anaesthetics. We are forced to do this or Victor will kill us. We are prisoners here."

Piper could not hold on to all this information.

"Let's check out the other buildings and then get out of here and get some help".

Zara hurried to the next shed. The big double doors were closed so they opened up a small side door and went in. This place had a central light on in the middle over a wire enclosure. Piper was distressed to see this because it was used for a vile and depraved purpose.

This was where the dogs were held by their owners in a face-off situation before being let go to fight. Often to the death. There were steps on either side for the punters to use a wooden balcony to view the entertainment. Wooden easels were propped up for bet taking.

The dogs used for fighting were caged at the far end of the barn and they were restlessly padding up and down while barking aggressively. Piper could see a German shepherd, several staffies, rottweilers and mastiffs all desperate to get out of their cages.

The girls were on different sides of the barn when Victor burst through the door and marched straight through. He was heading for the cages. Zara tiptoed up the steps and hid at the top. Piper had no choice but to retreat outside and decide where to go next. The sound of these dogs on the loose and coming her way forced her towards the remaining shed.

She hurried inside and shut the door quickly. She looked for a bolt to pull across but there was nothing. She stood facing the door for a long moment to get a grip on what was going on. She then turned around.

Chapter 23

Nothing had prepared her for the sight before her eyes. This wooden shed was lower than the other sheds and looked like a more recent build. Two camping lights were suspended from a long piece of electrical cable roughly tied to each end of the building.

The lamps produced enough light to see two rows of cages on either side of the building. Some were enclosed and some were open at the top. The size of each cage varied and in them were the saddest looking dogs she had ever seen. Dogs that looked worn out and defeated by their experiences.

In the first pen she passed, she saw a family of cockapoos. By their size, the pups were about four weeks old and were shades of gold and brown. They were all nestled into the mother who looked wretched and seriously underweight.

The floor of the cage was covered with straw that was soiled in places. Whoever was in charge had attempted to make a bed by using a large jumper.

A margarine container had been filled with drinking water and plastic ready meal trays used for dried food. Someone had been trying to help these poor animals but did not have the resources needed.

Piper presumed it was Sofi.

Piper walked up one side and down the other and found out that the pens contained mothers with pups, pregnant mums to be and at the back of the shed, a row of cages similar to those found in the previous barn and she presumed these contained the stud dogs. There was a chocolate labrador, a Biscon Frise, a cockapoo, a spaniel, a Staffordshire bull terrier, a Siberian husky and a small dachshund. They all looked like they had seen better days except the dachshund who still had some spirit left in his stance and a sparkle in his eyes.

Piper realised that the lamps could be slid along the cable to get the strongest light to a chosen spot. In the middle of one row, the cage had been opened out and four paving stones provided a firm foundation for a portable gas heater. One of the three sections was lit but it was still freezing cold conditions for the young pups.

As Piper stood to warm her hands and take in what she was viewing, she looked into the pen of an adult golden retriever and her one pup. She seemed to be fast asleep but the pup was desperately kneading her teat to find milk. Piper slid one of the lamps across the pen and realised that the mother was dead. She could not see any sign of breathing. There were no chest movements either. Piper put one foot into the cage, bent over and touched the dog's face. It was cold and rigid.

She then picked the young pup up, unzipped her snowsuit and opened her shirt. She lifted up her sports bra and put the pup inside the left cup and pulled the zip up to fix him more securely. She would have to find milk now. The sound of the barn door opening stopped her in her tracks and she immediately felt for the taser gun in her pocket.

"Piper, are you in here?"

"Yes, I hid from the dogs that Victor released."

Zara walked into the light and Piper was shocked to see that the large german shepherd was beside her.

"Is he friendly?"

"He is to me, he's my best boy but Victor locked me away from him."

Piper carefully laid the gun at the bottom of her pocket and remembered she still had small bottles of milk in the suit's other pockets. She had brought them for the little boy.

"Zara, the golden retriever mum is dead. She had one pup that I have stashed away in my jacket to keep warm. I still have the small bottles of milk we used to stabilise your son when we found him. I'll see if I can feed him."

Piper sat on the edge of one of the paving stones and took out one of the prepared bottles. She lifted the tab to warm the milk and pulled down her zip until a little head appeared. Without moving him she tried to put the teat in his mouth.

At first she was unsuccessful but after she moistened it in her own mouth the pup gradually started to suckle.

"Are you shocked by what you see?" asked Zara.

"Yes I am. Thank goodness for you and Sofi. These animals would be in a worse situation without you."

"Vincent gets the boys to steal dogs as well. The stud dogs are the lucky ones. They are set free afterwards.
The mothers stay until they are worn out and die.
"Can you walk the dogs that stay here?"
"We try to but it is hard for Sofi by herself."
"Where do you think she is?"
"I think she is in the house looking for blankets and bowls to help the dogs. If Vincent is outside, she sneaks in."
Piper noticed that the German shepherd was lying quietly by Zara.
"He doesn't look like a fighter."
"Vincent wants to use him in the ring. If not, he'll get rid of him.
Piper's pup had drunk himself to sleep so she zipped him back up.
"The helicopter should be back now. Shall we go. The quicker we go, the quicker we can get help."

"I will just find something to cover Sulaf before we go. She can rest in peace now. "
When she had finished, they walked over to the door.
"What is your beautiful boy called," asked Piper.
"Tartus, I will be sad to leave him. I hope he will be alright."
"He will be. He's coming with us. I just hope he likes helicopters."

Chapter 24

Piper peeked around the edge of the door to see if there were any humans or dogs outside but she saw no one. She beckoned to Zara to follow but fell over something large and heavy before she had walked five paces.
"It's the bottom of a fork lift truck. Just dumped there. Are you okay?" asked Zara.

Piper had fallen on her hands and knees and was relieved that she had not hurt the puppy. She would have to be more careful.

The two young women and Tartus crossed the yard and through the gate into the field. The helicopter was there and 2Sheds was sitting in the pilot's seat. Piper thought he would be there and had hoped it would have been someone else. She knew he would give her a hard time for recklessly staying behind.

He got out of the helicopter when he saw Zara.

"This is the little boy's mother. Have you any news for her 2Sheds?" asked Piper.

"Is he alive?" asked Zara.

"I checked on him before I came back and I was told that he was responding well to treatment."

Zara grasped 2Shed's hand and thanked him."

"What did John say? asked Piper anxiously. Has he contacted the emergency services to get out to this terrible place?"

2Sheds had been smiling at Zara but his expression changed when he turned to Piper.

"It's all under control and they are on their way. So can we go now?" he answered stiffly.

Piper did not have time to answer because she heard someone shouting Zara's name. She turned to see a young woman frantically clambering through the snow.

"It's my sister Sofi," cried out Zara.

"Please, you must help! He has petrol and is going to burn the sheds down. Come please.

2Sheds hadn't got a clue what was unfolding but Piper did. She unzipped her suit and took out the puppy and handed him to Zara.

"Show me" and she started to run. She was like a bat out of hell as she raced back to the farm yard. As she passed through the gate, she took the taser gun out of her pocket and held it out in front of her.

Piper saw Victor Saloman walking down to the bottom barn. He was not alone. A tall man was with him and he was carrying two jerry cans. Victor was carrying a heavy looking holdall in one hand and a gun in the other.

"Oh no you bloody don't Victor," yelled Piper and ran straight for him like someone possessed.

Victor Salomon stopped and raised his gun. He looked straight at his attacker and immediately froze. He knew that voice. He knew that face with long blonde hair flowing behind it. She was the stuff of his nightmares and with a scream of pure fear, he put both his hands over his ears and sank to his knees. The strap of the holdall fell forward, exposing his neck and for the second time in her life, Piper stood over him and this time fired the taser into his neck.

He shrieked with pain and then became perfectly still. She pulled the handcuffs out of her pocket and looked up for some help. Sofi was beside her.
" Help me pull him up to this truck base and we can cuff him to it."
They raised his arms above his head and cuffed him to a metal bar welded at both ends to the chassis of the truck. He wasn't going anywhere but Piper still cuffed his feet together as well.

So overwrought was Piper during this chaos that she had not even registered that Salomon had fired his gun into the air. Nor did she realise that the tall skinny man had dropped the cans and had run away into the darkness.

2Sheds had been a few minutes behind Piper because he had helped Zara and Tartus into the back of the helicopter but he had seen enough. He had seen Piper run straight at the man with the gun aimed at her.

He thought that he would see her gunned down but against all odds it didn't happen. Nevertheless 2Sheds was in a state of extreme agitation and he grabbed hold of Piper and shook her like a rag doll. Sofi tried to pull him off but she couldn't. When he eventually stopped, he pushed her to the floor and said,

"I never want to see you again."

And he was gone. He stormed back to the helicopter and flew out of Piper's life.

Chapter 25

" You didn't deserve that," said Sofia, as she helped Piper to her feet. "You were very brave."

"Or very stupid. That's what he will think." She took a long hard look at Victor Salomon. The man who had made her life a nightmare on Juniper Island. His eyes were shut as he sat there on a dry piece of ground under the shelter.

She had whipped off the strap on the holdall when she cuffed him. Now she looked inside the fat bulging bag to see numerous plastic bags full of what she presumed to be cocaine. Bundles of banknotes were hurriedly stuffed in as well. Piper zipped up the bag and left it beside him. The police could sort that out when they arrived.

When she had been in the third shed earlier, she had noticed several waterproof horse blankets. She fetched one and threw it over him. She didn't want him to freeze to death. That would have been too easy. She also pulled the two darts out of his neck because she thought they may be doing long term damage. She wished she had read the manual in more detail.

Sofi picked up Victor's gun and passed it to Piper who slipped it behind a bag of straw inside the barn.

The dogs were quieter now, exhausted from all the commotion.

"What happens now?" asked Sofi.

"2Sheds will have already updated the ship's crew about latest developments. We already know that the emergency services are on their way and another helicopter will come back for us."

"What is your ship?"

"It is an international rescue service that sails wherever it is needed. We do not work for any government."

Piper did not take her eyes off of the captured man and she would not leave this place until the police drove in through the farm gates. He was not going to escape her again.

"Do you want to come back with me, Sofi? Or do you want to stay with the dogs?"

Sofi turned to face Piper, "I cannot stay here. I am illegal and the police will arrest me. I want the dogs to be safe though."

"At least they will have a better life than they have now. Do you want to go and see if they need anything before we go,"

Sofi went into the shed and Piper stood staring at Salomon and she saw his eyelids flutter. He was keeping his eyes closed on purpose. She felt in her pocket to check if the taser gun was there. Then she thought of 2Sheds and how disastrous this night had been for them. She knew their relationship was over and there would be no going back from this. She couldn't live her life and always be answerable to him. A woman's place was in the revolution not at the kitchen sink.

"Who are you?" Victor had spoken. Piper looked down at him, "The person who will stop you and your cruel evil ways," Victor's eyes were half open and his mouth hardly opened when he talked.

"How do you know me?" he said robotically with no expression in his voice.

"I have met you once before and you were cruel and evil then."

"I do not know this time you speak off but I dream of you."

"Well unfortunately that has never stopped you."

Piper did not want to continue this conversation because there was no point. She heard a noise and saw Sofi coming out of the shed. She was carrying the little dachshund that had been in the line of kennels .

"This is Fred and he used to keep me company during the long nights. He was a good boy and never left my side. May I take him with me please."

"Of course, I thought he looked a bit special when I saw him earlier." Piper stroked his silky ears.

She glanced down at Victor who was staring at her.

She turned to Sofi, "Would you go over to the field and wait for the helicopter. Tell the pilot that I am waiting for the police services to arrive and then I'll come straight across."

"Will you talk to them?" asked the young woman.

"If I did, I don't think they would let me go, so I'll disappear before they reach the yard. Evidence of what has been going on is all around."

"And that is why Victor was going to burn it all down." Sofi kicked him in the leg and walked off across the yard. Victor looked up.
"That wasn't me. I'm the sort who would cut your bloody ears off!"

Piper would stop there. She walked into the yard and stood some distance away. But not far enough to taser him again if the need arose.

Chapter 26

The line of emergency service vehicles looked like a silver and blue snake curling around the country lanes on its way to the farm. Piper had doggedly waited in the yard and rarely took her eyes off of the man who had caused so much harm, even in the short time she had known him.

His childhood friend Joram who was now her friend as well, had shocking stories to tell. What had been different for Joram was, even though he had suspected Victor, he had never actually witnessed any of these atrocities and always seemed to give him the benefit of the doubt.

True as her word, Piper slipped across the yard as soon as the police entered the property. She found Sofi and the pilot sitting in the chopper waiting for her. She had not met the pilot before. He seemed friendly and patient unlike 2Sheds and soon they were up in the air.

Piper looked down to see the yard swarming with people, some of whom held guns. She could see Victor being escorted away in handcuffs in between two tall policemen. She had forgotten about leaving the key to the cuffs but they seem to have quickly sorted that one. A policewoman carried the bulky holdall behind them.

She watched until they were out of sight and then carefully took the taser gun out of her pocket. She removed the cartridges and put them and the gun in the glove compartment. Sofi was now in the back seat with Fred who looked very excited. He was free and he was with Sofi. He had everything he needed.

The pilot was called Luke and looked like a young 2Sheds. He had unruly hair, bright eyes and a Roman nose. Just like 2Sheds!. This gave him a strongly defined profile.

Piper asked him if he knew any updates about the farm incident. He said that John had delved into police records for this area and had come up with some interesting details. There was already concern about a new drug doing the rounds but it had not been linked to the isolated farm.

"John also read several reports about dogs being stolen from their owners but little police action was taken. They did not link these abductions as being one perpetrator."

"And any suspicions on the dog fighting?" asked Piper.

"Not really but several comments about expensive cars being seen in the area every month. Still no links were being made to organised crime."

Piper looked behind to check on Sofi and found she was asleep with Fred lying over her lap.

The two front seat passengers went quiet and within the next hour, Piper could

see the four funnels of Abednego. She couldn't wait to be with Stanley.
It felt like she had been away much longer than one night. In fact she felt like she had been time travelling into the past for a long time. Back to Juniper Island.

    John Bartlebee and Stanley were waiting for them and her beautiful dog came rushing forward and was so pleased to see her that he pushed her over and she landed on her bottom. She held onto Stanley and could feel tears running down her face. Perhaps he had sensed her anguish because he didn't move. He just absorbed her distress.

    In the background, Piper could hear Luke introducing Sofi to John. She could hear John ask him to take Sofi to see her sister and her nephew. It sounded like the little boy was making a good recovery.

    When they had gone, he walked over to Piper, took her hands and pulled her up.

She stood and leaned into him sobbing uncontrollably.

"He hates me," was all she could say. He hugged her for a long time and then with his arm around her guided her to his den. By the time she was sitting on his big comfy settee, she was feeling more in control of herself. Stanley jumped up beside her and she felt safe. John went into the kitchen and returned with the tiny retriever puppy. He passed him over to Piper and she held him close to her chest.

"How's he doing?" she asked.

"Doc Roger says he is doing fine. We need to feed him every three hours."

Stanley was lifting his head and gently nudging the puppy to say that he was there.

"They're going to get on well" said John as Piper laid the pup on the thick mane of hair beside Stan's face.

The little body relaxed and was fast asleep by the time John came back with two mugs of tea.

"I haven't asked about the nitwits,"

"They're fine. Jack and Amalie, yikes I forgot !

I should have said Jack and Mary flew over from their home in Kingfisher when they heard you were coming here. They should all be fast asleep until the morning."

Piper felt emotional again at the thought of seeing her grandad and to change the subject, she asked him to tell her about his mission to Heaven.

"I bet Tom Cat missed you," she said.

"He stayed here with Daniel and his moggy and seems to have been fine. Cats are independent beasts and seem to cope with change."

Before settling down, John went into the kitchen to fetch a bottle of milk for the pup. Piper could see that the teat on this bottle was smaller and longer.

"Ah, I expect he likes that teat better." commented Piper.

John laughed, "HE doesn't but SHE does. That's another thing I've got wrong."

Piper looked slightly shocked but then burst out laughing.

John was pleased to hear her laugh. He picked up the pup and settled down to feed her, Stanley moved himself around and laid his head on Piper's lap.

"I'll begin at the beginning and try to fill in the details but just like 2Sheds in The Earth World, certain parts are very fuzzy and unclear to me now.

I received a visitor two days before I left here. I walked into my den to see a young man looking at the song titles on the jukebox. He was dressed in a pale green tunic, loose trousers and sand shoes. I suspected he was a messenger angel. He said his name was Jacob and he had an invitation for me to visit The Garden of Eden. He emphasised that there was nothing to be worried about. God was thankful for the work I did. That is when I asked 2Sheds to let you know that I would not be going to Gracious Palace with you.

And Piper thought of what happened on that visit and felt miserable all over again. The pup with no name had finished her milk and looked slightly drunk so John wrapped her in a small towel and passed him over to Piper to hold.

John took a drink of his tea and continued his story.

" Two days later, I was coming through the door of the den when it seemed to light up all around me and instead of coming in here, I walked into Eden. It looked, smelt and sounded divine. I could have stood in that moment forever. I felt intoxicated and totally happy and content.

Jacob was waiting for me and we walked across beautiful lush grass until we came to a stream with the freshest water gurgling over small pebbles. There was a group of heavenly people in the distance. I say heavenly because they seemed to emit a golden aura.

One of them instantly stood out and had the strongest aura of them all. He was tall and straight and looked like a North American Indian Chief. He had long, shiny black hair tied in a plait running down his back. As I stood in awe, his face seemed to be changing into Mother Teresa's. I do not know how long I stood there but I could clearly see the images of faces from all nations. He was all people in one.

As I listened to his voice, it was my voice.

I knew then for certain that we are all made in the same image and likeness and we are one with God."

John stopped and had a drink of his tea even though it must have been cold by now.

"I don't remember what happened next but I was back with Jacob who took me by the hand and we flew like birds to wonderful places. I saw rainforests surrounding cities of gold where man and beast lived in harmony. I could swim to the bottom of the ocean and walk along the sea bed without any breathing apparatus.

"Jacob took me to museums lined with silver and gold in which the absolute truth about humanity was recorded. Amongst the eternal works of art, the message was clear. God had not created evil.
Evil was what was left when goodness had been taken away.

John looked across at Piper and thought she looked overcome with awe and emotion. "Shall we stop there for now ?," he asked. "Please tell me how this affects your work on Abednego and then I'll sleep for a while."
"Okay, it is the issue that you and 2Sheds have been concerned about. Humans need the Earth experience to prepare them for eternity. It gives them the life choices

that shape their destiny. God did not create evil and cannot destroy it."
"Are you saying that I must go back?" blurted out Piper.
" You can choose what you would like to do but I have found out that if you do decide to go back, your family can go with you."
"But what about you know who?" She couldn't bear to say his name."
"He can go with you and always be with you but in other incarnations. That is your thank you gift from Heaven."
" I think I know about this", said Piper suddenly. Gramps told me about a man who had been a Japanese prisoner of war. He had been tortured and starved and when he eventually came home took a long time to recover. He was often seen walking his West Highland white terrier that he called Jock. For the rest of his life and he lived to a grand old age, he always had Jock by his side. Gramps said he probably had four different Jocks in his lifetime but I felt

very strongly that when one Jock died, the same one came back to him. "

John Bartlebee smiled at his daughter and believed what she had said,
"I think you know more than I do. Looks like we're already sorted Piper. I am so very proud of you. Let's get some sleep now and talk more in the morning."

Chapter 27

Piper woke up to see her beloved Gramps sitting opposite her, "I thought I'd just come over."
She knew then that John had spoken to him and she felt overcome with tears again. "2Sheds hates me," She surprised herself by saying it again. A lot more important things had happened. But he had been so angry with her. She started to cry and Jack came over and squeezed in beside her.

He put his arm around her and she buried her head on his chest,

Piper cried for a long time and Gramps held her tight. "Let it all out my sweet one, you've had a lot to deal with."

Eventually she stopped and Jack made her some tea and toast. He also fed Stanley.

"John has taken Rosie to see the doc. He shouldn't be long."

"Who?" asked Piper, wiping away her tears.

"The poor little pup without a name," he answered.

"I didn't even know she was a little girl. Is she ok?"

"We're just making sure. John thought he might have been a bit hasty taking her out of the medical centre."

"He probably did that for me. Did you know that I'm going back to The Earth World Gramps?"

"Yes, John did tell me and it's wonderful news about Stanley."

"I forgot to ask about Calico. She might be genetically a Gracious Angel."

"No it's alright. John told me that she's only about 5%. The majority is white European.

"I wonder if she'll want to go,"

"What ? To the home of Mary Poppins ? She'll love it."

At that moment, John returned with the newly named Rosie. Stanley got up right away and nuzzled his face into the puppy's body. John gently lay her in the big dog's mouth and he brought her over to Piper.

"Doc says she's fine considering what she's been through. He gave me some medication to clear her digestive system from any infections that could be lurking."

Jack stood up and looked a bit uncomfortable. He turned to his companions, "Tell me if I'm interfering but I was thinking that this might be a good time to talk about where you would live back in The Earth World."

"What about the nitwits? I ought to go and see them," said Piper , starting to get up.

"Stay there a minute, we won't be able to talk about this in their company, so why don't we sort things out now. I thought I would take Rosie and some bottles of milk over to the cabin. Mary will make sure she is in safe hands. That will give us the opportunity to thrash this out and have something to work towards."

"If we are going to do this, we do it now and put us all out of our misery," agreed John.

"Okay then," said Piper, passing Rosie to Jack.

"I won't be long, By the time you've made a cuppa, I'll be back.

Jack took the puppy and his milk and was gone, Piper took Stan out on the deck to stretch his legs and within ten minutes, they were all back together again.

"Calico was a bit tearful to see such a young puppy," said Jack. She couldn't get over how tiny she was.

"She can be a sensitive soul." added Piper.

John came in with refreshments and they all sat back in their seats.

"Another saga I'm afraid, but this time I'll try to make it brief and succinct," said John.

Over the years, I have been on Abednego, we have managed to buy some properties in The Earth World. We use them as halfway houses for our families. One of these places is a farm in Wales that we bought at the time that I found out that I had a daughter and I put it in your name. There's a lot of behind the scenes jiggery pokery that goes on but no single person is robbed. We choose properties that are empty because the owners have died and have no family. "What do you think Piper?"

"Is it run down? I'm not sure I would be any good at DIY." asked Piper, looking overwhelmed.

"Definitely not. The farmhouse is an old stone building which has been renovated and modernised.
Two of our Syrian refugee families have built themselves houses on the site and started to cultivate the land. Sheep are kept in the neighbouring fields. It could be quite an enterprising community."
"What do you think, Gramps? The whole thing makes me want to ball my eyes out." She looked away in an attempt to control the flow of tears.

Jack put his cup down and came to sit on the arm of her chair. He put his arm around the back of it,
"I don't understand the logistics of how this is done. I've read of estates that have lain empty for many years even falling into

neglect. I've also heard of huge amounts of money stashed away in banks all over The Earth World and never used. If the clever people of The Lysie World can use this for a good purpose, I do not see the harm in it."

"I know that I must do this but I am finding it incredibly hard," she cried and the tears started flowing.

John stood up and fetched his laptop. He turned it on and accessed a video link. Piper could hear a cheerful woman's voice and children playing in the background. He put the laptop on her knee and paused the video,

"This is Dani. She is living in Skylark's Farm with her family. She is going to take you on a whirlwind tour and facetime you later if you would like that."

Piper placed the laptop so that her grandad could see the screen as well. She pressed play and a young Syrian woman, possibly about the same age as Piper came into sight. She had long wavy black hair tied in a ponytail and was wearing a black t-shirt and jeans. She was standing outside the door of stone built house,

"Hi Piper, I don't know if you remember me but we started an A level course together on Abednego. I don't think either of us finished it though. I didn't because I came here to live with my husband Caleb. We now have two children.

"Do you remember her?" asked Jack.

"Yes I do, we both found the Thomas Hardy book we were studying rather hard going. She was nice."

By now Dani was inside the house and walking from room to room giving a guided tour. Upstairs in one of the bedrooms, she filmed the view from the window. It was impressive with a variety of chickens and ducks in the yard. The land behind them was divided into a large agricultural area with well established hedges dividing the different areas. There were also sheds and a few greenhouses. The fruit and vegetables looked healthy and abundant.

Piper could see two new builds beyond the gardens which presumably belonged to the two families. Beyond that were green fields with an abundance of sheep.

Piper realised she had not been listening to poor Dani who was doing a great job of describing this attractive homestead. Piper tuned back in time to hear Dani say that this breed of sheep produced fleeces which were perfect for knitting wool. She hoped Piper might have some ideas of how to use this asset to their advantage.

The video clip was coming to an end and Dani gave a farewell wave of her hand. Piper shut the laptop and stood up,
"I think that I had better go and see Doc Roger and get something to dry up the tears. I know it's what I have to do and the farm looks lovely. It also looks like I need to learn to knit."

"Shall I come with you?" asked Jack.
" No thanks Gramps, time for me to get a grip and realise how blessed I am."
She kissed him on the cheek and with Stanley by her side, she went to find Doc Roger. The refreshing sea air hit her as she walked down to the main deck.
She remembered the first time she had walked along here and half expected to see Kate Winslet and Leo DeCaprio. It was then that she first experienced Abednego splitting the scene in front of her to enter The Earth World.
Piper enjoyed walking around the deck with her beloved boy. She was beginning to feel better.

    She found Doc Roger sitting beside the cot of a little girl who had recently been rescued from a horrific home situation where she had been repeatedly kicked and punched by the people looking after her. She was called Skye and had tubes, wires and cables attaching her little body to various machines. Piper could see bruises on her arms, neck and face.

"Skye looked like she had been in a car accident," said the doc when he saw Piper." I can't believe a person could do this to a small defenceless child."

Piper felt outrage in her soul. She had previously read the reports of what had happened, "If I am to return to The Earth World, I will look after her and dedicate my days to help her overcome this ."

"That would be a wonderful solution. I am surprised to hear that you agreed to go back."

"That's partly why I'm here. I think I need some medication to dry up the tears that I keep dissolving into. Seeing Skye has strengthened my resolve but I have been so useless up till now. I shouldn't be and I have probably been ungrateful because Stanley is coming with me. How blessed is that ! Then again, I wonder if I should take him and Calico from a perfect life to one that is far from perfect."

A nurse came along to sit with the little girl so Doc Roger stood up and putting his arm around Piper's shoulders walked back to his office. Stanley followed, hoping there might be a flapjack in it for him. Piper sat down while the doctor went into a side room where he kept a stock of medication for quick and easy access.

He brought out three blister packs of small white tablets.
"I'm not so sure I need them now. Seeing Skye puts everything into proportion."
"When are you thinking of going?"
"Tomorrow, I can't bear thinking about it any longer."
"In that case, I'll take those back and give you something more immediate."
Doc Roger went out and came back with a syringe and hypodermic needle,

" This will be better for you. A medication that will give you a boost to get through the next few days."

Piper held out her arm and the doc administered the medication.
"Okay?" he asked"
"I am now. She looked at him with a sudden puzzled expression. "I've just realised something. I do not know your surname. Everybody always calls you Doc Roger."
"That is my surname," he smiled mischievously.
"Then I do not know your christian name." She was beginning to realise there was a mystery here.
"My full name is Docton Roger. No middle name.
In the fifteenth century the de Docton family owned a large estate in North Devon. They even had their own coat of arms."
"And I never knew you had such a distinguished family history. Well thank

you for the chat and the jab. It feels like it's done the trick. I had better go and see my little nitwits. They might think I'm avoiding them."

"Hang on and I'll come with you and check out the pup and I think Stanley (his ears pricked up !) deserves a flapjack (his saliva glands started to work !)"

"You had better hurry up or we'll need to mop the floor." laughed Piper.

Chapter 28

Calico was sitting quietly watching a children's programme on the television when Piper walked into her rooms on Abednego and Mary was helping Rafi bottle feed the pup on the settee. She had paper towels ready for any toilet activity.

Piper was surprised that Calico did not jump up to see her. In fact she thought the little girl looked sad.

After ruffling Rafi's hair and saying hello to Mary, Piper picked up Calico and sat down with her on her lap. She whispered in her ear,
"What's the matter with you boo boo?" and cuddled her into her body.
"I didn't think you were coming back. I thought you had gone back to live in The Earth World."
She's overheard something, thought Piper.
"If I was going back to live there, I would take you all with me."
The four year old wriggled around and looked up at Piper "Do you promise?"
"Yes I most certainly do."
The door opened and John Bartlebee and Jack came into the room.
"We are going to live in The Earth World," shouted Calico.
"Wow, that was quick," said John looking across to Piper.
"Calico was sad when I came back. She thought I had left her.

Doc Roger gently took the pup from Rafi.
"Can Rosie come too?" asked the little boy.
"Sounds like it's all decided," added Mary.
Piper looked at her grandad. He was looking sad so she passed Calico over to John and went over to her beloved Gramps. She held his arm,
"Gramps, if I don't go now, I'll never go. It's the worst thing I have ever done."
Jack put his arms around her, kissed her on her head, stifled a sob and left the room.
"I'll go after him," said Doc Roger. "Bye guys. I know you'll rock it."

Dear sweet Mary got up and went to every member of Piper's family and held their faces and kissed them on the cheek. Lastly she kissed Piper and hugged her,
"Till we meet again my darling girl,"

This had all gone far too quick for John, who looked visibly shaken. "Is this it?" he asked weakly.

Piper walked into the kitchen and he followed, "I saw Skye in the hospital and her plight has changed everything for me. I would like to dedicate my new life to making it up to that little girl for the vile things that have happened to her. Would that be possible?"

John thought for a long moment, "Yes it is possible but it will be quite a while before she is ready to leave the hospital."

"That will give me time to settle back into the hardships of life on Earth. But I will always be committed to helping those who are persecuted and unable to fight back."

John pulled Piper to him, "I am very proud of you and wish I could have been a better father to you."

They stayed together for a while and then John attempted an upbeat voice,

"I'll go and pick up all the paperwork which you need to look through. It will contain medical history originating in Manchester. Things changed after the head injury and this can be your 'get out of jail' card because there will be things you simply don't remember."

"I will read it all many times. I'm thinking of going tomorrow. Our bags are still packed from Gratitude and I need to get it over and done with. Just one more question."

She looked him straight in the eyes. "What about 2Sheds? Will he be told where we have gone?"

John looked prepared for this answer, " No and likewise you will not know where he has gone. That is presuming he goes back. I think he will and will set up home with Crosby. I think we will leave everything else up to destiny. Give you both a fresh start and if it is meant to be, you will unknowingly find each other again. Is that alright with you Piper?"

Piper put her face in her hands and massaged her forehead,

"Yep, I feel lost without him but we blew it, didn't we?"

John did not answer. He gave her a kiss on her cheek and walked away. The next time she saw him, he had a briefcase full of legal documents,
"I've arranged for the helicopters to take you and your belongings over tomorrow morning. I'll see you before you leave.
"Bloody hell Pops, this is unbearable.

Chapter 29

By mid morning of the following day, Piper was sitting in a helicopter leaving Abednego for the very last time. She sat in the front with Patch curled up in the footwell and Rosie the puppy on her lap. Stanley, Rafi and Calico sat in the back.

She had not seen John before she left because it had been too upsetting for both of them. Now she would gradually forget him and the adventures that had befallen her. She remembered the first time she had ever seen him. He had been in the wheelhouse looking out to sea and singing the James song,

'Sit down next to me' as he guided the enormous ship to The Lysie Fields. She thought he was so gorgeous with his unruly curly hair and could easily have been a rockstar.

    Piper stopped herself reminiscing. She was pleased to find that the helicopter pilot was the young man who had flown her back to the ship from Victor Saloman's farm. That seemed like months ago instead of a couple of days. Oh, how her life had changed. She looked down at the footwell where Patch was fast asleep. She remembered the box with the taser in it and she suddenly felt miserable about the whole experience and how furious 2Sheds had been. Soon she would have also forgotten him.

"Have you been keeping up with the Earth news? Sounds like the remains of human bodies have been found in the incinerator."

"What incinerator?" said Piper, startled at the pilot's words."

"The incinerator they used for the dead fighting dogs."

Piper shuddered. At least she had put a stop to that."And what happened to the man I tasered?"

"He will be going to prison for a very long time. He was involved in the production of drugs, dog fights involving large sums of money, breeding puppies like chickens lay eggs. And now murder."

"Murder of the poor illegal immigrants he forced to work for him I expect," added Piper.

"Well this case will continue for a long time. He can't have been working alone. You deserve a medal for what you did."

"I didn't want him to burn the place down, that's all I thought of at the time."
Piper turned around and Calico was cuddled into Stanley.
She was fast asleep and so was Rafi.
Back on Abednego, Doc Roger was writing up his medical notes in his office when he felt a presence at the door. He looked up to see John Bartlebee standing at the door,
"I guess I need a jab like the one you gave Piper. I feel like I've lost my mojo and need to be scrapped up off the floor."
The doc stopped what he was doing, stood up and walked over to John,
" Come with me and I'll show you what sorted Piper's melancholy."
The two men walked into the intensive care unit and stopped beside the cot of Skye,
"By the time Piper heard about this little girl's injuries and the way she had been used as a punchbag, she forgot about her

own sadness and forged a decision to make things better for Skye."

"But what about the jab you gave her?"

"That was a vaccine to protect her against Earth's new ailments. They are just coming out of a Covid pandemic."

"Did she know?"

"I planned to tell her before she boarded the helicopter but Skye took a turn for the worse and I was called away. It's nothing to worry about as she won't remember any of it in a couple of days anyway, so no harm has been done."

"And she was strong enough to brave it out herself. If she can do it, so can I. Thanks Doc, I'll see you later.

Back on Juniper Island, 2Sheds was playing tennis with Crosby in the courts that Ty Clay and Piper had discovered. He thought of her a hundred times a day.

" I never want to see you again," that was a terrible thing to say, especially when she had been desperate to save those dogs from a terrifying death.

Crosby was just about to carry out an underarm serve, when Marigold and Maya ran onto the court.

"Steady on, what's so important," said 2Sheds as the two girls nearly ran into him.

"It's Piper, she has gone to live in The Earth World," said Marigold.

2Sheds could not believe his ears. His first words were,

"But what about Stanley?"

"He was allowed to go as well. They have all gone," added Maya.

"How do you know this?" asked 2Sheds in disbelief.

"Joram just told us," they said simultaneously and then froze. Perhaps they should not have told 2Sheds in such an excitable manner.

2Sheds passed over the tennis racquet to Marigold,

"Can you take over the game? I need to make a phone call."

"I won't be long," he shouted to Crosby, who was patiently waiting on the other side of the net.

2Sheds left the court and walked up the lane that Ty Clay had cleared over eighteen months ago. How things had changed. He came out at the top and sat on the bench opposite. He rang John who picked up on the fourth ring.

"Hi John, I've just been told that Piper has returned to The Earth World. Why didn't you let me know?"

"I wanted to but you had blocked my calls, so I asked Joram to tell you."

2Sheds realised that he had done this on the evening he had returned to Juniper Island. He didn't want to talk to anyone as he had been so angry. Well, he had shot himself in the foot by doing that.

John was still talking, "I think we need to chat about this in person, don't you?"

"Yeah, I just need to get my head around this. When did she go?"

"Early this morning. I had no idea that it would have happened so quickly."

"And you won't tell me where she has gone?"

"You know I can't do that."

2Sheds finished the call and sat with his head in his hands for a long time with the words, 'I don't want to see you any more' ringing in his ears.

At the same time Jack Lee, his wife Mary and their little black dog Alice were in a helicopter returning to their hometown of Kingfisher. They were quiet, lost in thoughts of Piper and her crazy little family. They would sorely miss them.

At one point, Mary leant forward to speak to the pilot, "Could we please stop off at Rainbow Bridge for a while."

"Yes of course, I'll just punch in the new route. Should be there in an hour."

"Feels like Alice could do with a new friend?" said Mary.

"Sounds like a good idea for all of us," agreed Jack, putting his arm around his wife.

Two hours later, they were back in the helicopter heading for home. Alice was lying on Jack's lap with her head resting on Mary's knee because there sat a black fluffy puppy sitting up proudly looking at Alice.

"She's a little beauty," said the pilot, turning around in his seat to admire her.

"Her name is Peggy and she is a labradoodle pup. She was born in The Earth World to a labrador whose owner did not know his working dog was pregnant. When he found the litter, he removed the mother and left the puppies to die. They entered Rainbow Bridge where they have been nurtured and reared. Now she will live with us and be Alice's forever friend.

Chapter 30

Two years down the road found Piper and her family attending their first Glastonbury. They pitched their tents in the traders campsite just behind The Green Fields. Piper had thrown herself into the production of wool since taking up residence on the farm. She was surprised to find out that her herd of sheep were a rare breed called Cotswolds and produced sturdy, shiny wool that was suitable for outdoor wear as well as home textiles like blankets.

That was enough to motivate Piper. She liked these calm and friendly animals. They were long in length and tall in height with a lustrous fleece which resembled white dreadlocks. The dreadlocks seemed so familiar but she could not remember the significance of them. Maybe it was from Calico, whose hair needed a lot of combing as it seemed to easily become knotted.

The first year was a steep learning curve for her. The two Syrian families had already been looking after this flock of sheep for several years previously and had been successful in keeping them happy and healthy. They had already decided not to kill the sheep for meat. Every year they had sheared the sheep and sold the fleeces to the mill.

Piper wanted to pursue the idea of selling their own wool and making their own garments. She learnt how to knit and with Dani learnt how to make blankets on a hand operated knitting machine. She came up with her first range of colours that were inspired by the sea glass colours that she found on the beach.

The names for each specific colour came so easily to her and she was surprised by that. There was juniper green, kingfisher blue, greysand, sandstone pink, seaglass red ……………

The tone was weather beaten and muted. Piper had read that British wool could be produced regeneratively, processed simply and result in wool that was good to wear and good for the planet. They worked to encourage wildlife habitats and improve the soil. It all sounded exciting but she did realise that there would be a lot to learn. Presumably there would be issues with not killing her sheep and possibly how many years did the sheep produce quality fleeces.

   But at the moment, they were flying high. Their pitch seemed popular on Green Fields. It had large, laminated photos around a stall selling skeins of wool, blankets, scarves and plenty of woolly jumpers. The photos depicted the different stages of the yearly process from lambing to shearing and to the wool preparation at the mill. Visitors could also watch blankets being made on the knitting machine.

When they shut up shop in the evening, Dani and her family went straight down to the concert stages but Piper would take the nitwits and Stanley back to their tent behind Green Fields. She shared her tent with Kismet, who was Rafi's biological mother.

One of the first things that Piper did on coming to live in Wales was to search for Rafi's family. She could not remember or understand why she had not done that before. After six months of searching, she found out that Kismet was the sole survivor of his family and was living in Turkey. Piper made contact with her through the United Nations Refugee Agency and she arrived for the family's first Christmas in Wales.

Piper talked with Rafi who was seven years old now and told him everything that he needed to know.

He had thought all his family were dead and thought it was wonderful that she was still alive. Piper reassured him that nothing would change in their life if he didn't want it too and that was exactly how things panned out. Kismet came to live in the family house and Rafi became Rafi 2Mums, which made him laugh although yet again Piper felt the name was familiar to her.

    Piper and Kismet became friends and shared a keen interest in the craft side of their wool business. At the festival, they took it in turns staying with the nitwits while one was free to go and listen to the music. It was Paul McCartney on the Pyramid Stage that night so Kismet who was planning to watch Diana Ross on the Sunday afternoon, would be nitwit-sitting. Piper remembered listening to The Beatles with her grandad when she was a little girl. She was sure that Paul would play some old favourites.

While they were at Glastonbury, Hassan and Amira, who also lived on the farm, stayed behind in Wales. They had two sons and a border collie who had taken easily to gathering and controlling the sheep. His best friend was Rosie, the golden retriever puppy who was now two years old. The two dogs worked the sheep together and it was no hardship for Rosie to stay on the farm.

Patch also stayed behind. A year ago Piper had searched out a female friend for him and she was now pregnant with his foal. They now had their own stable with all the trimmings.

Beside their tent at Glastonbury, was a family who made and sold wicker produce on one side and on the other, a tent full of young men who were working for The Ocean Cleanup. This organisation's aim was to clean up the oceans and rivers of plastic. A massive task. Piper had noticed their large tent in The Green Fields and was pleased to see so many people of all ages attending the meetings and taking interest in the new technologies being used.

The organisation had two main aims. One was to stop plastic being dumped into the rivers and seas. Two was to clean up what was already there before it broke down so small that it would be extremely hard to remove.

Most evenings their tent was quiet and the men would not return until the early hours. That night they were there and Piper could hear them playing music and enjoying themselves. They were all in their twenties with beards and hair or beards and no hair. They all sported Ocean Cleanup t-shirts. She lay back in her deck chair and closed her eyes and listened to their music drifting in the air and smelt the herbs and spices of festival food.

Kismet was sitting with Calico showing her how to knit on a simple loom and Rafi was shelling peas for a salad. She heard a loud 'oooohhhhh' and a thud on the ground.

Stanley, who had been watching Rafi, barked and ran past him. Piper opened her eyes to see Stan lying on top of a man who was flat on the ground holding a frisbee high in the air. The nitwits ran up to them and were jumping around and whooping in excitement.

    Piper pushed herself out of the deckchair. Stanley's tail was sweeping backwards and forwards like a manic windscreen wiper,
"Stanley, get off. What are you doing?" She put her arms around his neck and pulled him off but he still wanted to get back to the poor man who was trying to get up.
"I am so sorry, it looks like my family think they know you. I don't know why they are so excited." said Piper, wringing her hands stressfully. She just hoped the guy was not going to be annoyed.

"It's 2Sheds," sang Calico as she danced around the poor man who was wiping Stanley slobber off his face,
"Kismet, can you take the nitwits inside for a cold drink please?"
Kismet did as she was asked and Piper was left alone with Stanley who was totally unaware that he might be in trouble. He was just smiling and gazing at the man as if he was a superstar. His tail was still in hyperdrive.
"Bloody hell, that was some welcome," said the young man who did not appear to be injured or annoyed.
"I have never seen him do anything like that before," Piper said apologetically. "I'm so sorry. Would you like a bottle of pear cider? It's been chilling in the fridge."

The man who looked about Piper's age looked over at his mates but they seemed to have lost interest in the frisbee and were now stretched out on the grass soaking up the sun.

" Good idea, thanks."

Piper let go of Stanley who just stood happily beside this person. She went inside and came out with two opened bottles.

"Take a seat," she said politely as she plonked herself down in the seat she had previously been sitting on. He sat down beside her and she passed over a bottle. He drank eagerly.

"That's better," he said.

"But even the nitwits were over the moon to see you." Piper said feeling relieved that all was well.

He laughed,"That's unusual terminology. And what were they calling me?"

"It sounded like two sheds but I'm not sure.

It wasn't anything I can relate to," answered Piper taking her first drink from the cold bottle.

"That is strange because my name is Eric Touchette and when some people pronounce it, it does sound like Eric 2Shed."

"But this can only be a coincidence," She replied. "And by the way I'm Piper Lee."
"Well Piper Lee, it's been the strangest way of meeting someone, maybe part of the Glastonbury magic."
She noticed he had finished his pear cider and went to get another bottle. When she came back, Stanley was sitting beside Eric proudly holding the tatty old blue Converse boot he took everywhere with him,
"Is that my boot?" he joked. "I used to have blue converse boots."
"He has had it for years," laughed Piper. "I can't remember where he got it from."
She passed him the bottle and sat down.
"I'm beginning to feel dumped. Stanley has never been so fascinated with anyone like he is with you."
Eric leant forward and rubbed the top of the dog's head.
"He certainly is a beauty. Have you had him since he was a puppy?"

"Not quite, in fact I'm not sure when I had him. I had a head injury when I was sixteen and there are lots of gaps in my memory." Piper settled back in her deckchair with her own drink.

"That's awful for you. Are you okay now?"

" Yes, ever since I've been living in Wales and that's two years now. I wonder if my new life of keeping sheep and using their wool for making clothes has helped. My life is more stable now.

"I'm a bit the same. I was left on a remote beach by my parents when I was a baby. I was carefully wrapped up warm and shielded by a wind break.

I think my grandfather was supposed to find me but I found out recently that he had been killed in nearby woods.

"Bloody hell, what a terrible thing to happen," exclaimed Piper, trying not to have such an astonished look on her face and trying to keep her mouth closed.

"It is generally thought that my parents drowned as they attempted to swim to safety. Their bodies were never found."

"But who found you?" asked Piper incredulously.

"Some modern day pirates and I stayed with them until my late teens. It was then I found out that I was heir to my grandfather's estate and so I sold up and came to England and I am in my second year at university in Plymouth studying marine biology.

I also volunteer with The Ocean Cleanup."

Piper had been watching him as he talked about himself. Strangely their life histories seemed similar.

"Looks like we're both been lost sheep in our past," she said thoughtfully.

"I wonder if our paths have crossed but I'm certain I would have remembered you," he said.

It was at that point that Eric's five mates appeared at the edge of the tent pitch,

"We're on our way to see Mr McCartney. Are you coming?" shouted the one with a long beard and no hair.

"Yea I'm coming." Eric looked down at Stanley,

"Looks like I need to get up, Stan. It's been great meeting you." As he got up, the beautiful dog gave a cry of disappointment and went to sit beside Piper, who put her arm around him.

"I hope you enjoy your evening and thanks for the pear ciders."

And with a wave of his hand he was gone. It was quite dark now and Piper lit the camping lights and sat back in her deck chair. She closed her eyes because she wanted to think over her meeting with Eric Touchette and the strange reactions from her faithful dog and the nitwits.

She had thought he was very good looking with his unruly brown hair, twinkling eyes and rugged features. He was one of the six with hair and a beard.

She thought of their conversation and what she had learnt of his past and how alike they were; they both shared similar experiences. He had been separated from his family and grew up in an unstable environment. He also had come out of it with an inheritance.

Piper wondered if she would see him again. She put her hand down on Stan's back and ran her fingers down his fur and started to drift off. Stanley stood up and she could feel the draft from his tail wagging.

She opened her eyes and Eric was there gently cupping the dogs face in his hands, "I wondered if you wanted to come and see the main man with me?" he asked hopefully. "Have you come all the way back to ask me?" she replied, looking straight back at him."

Eric crouched down and held on to both sides of her deckchair, "I got there and I was missing you, so I came back to get you."

"You had better tell Stan," she said.

"He won't mind, it was his idea," he replied.

Piper jumped up,"I'll get my jumper."

She felt excited,"I won't be long Stan. You look after the nitwits for me."

Stanley picked up the baseball boot and went into the tent and lay down just inside the entrance. Piper put on her jumper and kissed her beautiful dog on the nose. She ran after Eric Touchette without a care in the world. A group of Paul McCartney fans in front of them were singing Hey Jude and she joined in with them.

"That's not our song," he said and broke into

> I've just seen a face
> I can't forget the time or place
> Where we just met
> She's just the girl for me

And I want all the world to see we've met......"

Piper put her arm through his and joined in the chorus

"Fallin', yes I am falling

And she keeps callin'

Me back again."

Back at the tent, Stanley got up and walked out onto the path between the tents. He followed at a distance with the converse boot in his mouth. He stopped and watched them walk out of sight.

With his beautiful tail swaying to and fro, he walked back. He passed a cardboard box half full of rubbish and stopped to drop the converse boot inside.

He did not need it any more.